THE
INFLUENCED

Maya, never lose sight of your own vision!
Khadija

KHADIJA GRANT

Disclaimer

No part of this publication may be reproduced or transmitted in any form or by any means, mechanical or electronic, including photocopying or recording, or by any information storage and retrieval system, or transmitted by email without permission in writing from the publisher.

While all attempts have been made to verify the information provided in this publication, neither the author nor the publisher assumes any responsibility for errors, omissions, or contrary interpretations of the subject matter herein.

This book is for entertainment purposes only. The views expressed are those of the author alone, and should not be taken as expert instruction or commands. The reader is responsible for his or her own actions.

Adherence to all applicable laws and regulations, including international, federal, state and local governing professional licensing, business practices, advertising, and all other aspects of doing business in the US, Canada or any other jurisdiction is the sole responsibility of the purchaser or reader. Neither the author nor the publisher assume any responsibility or liability whatsoever on the behalf of the purchaser or reader of these materials. Any perceived slight of any individual or organization is purely unintentional.

DEDICATIONS

To my husband, who sacrificed so much to allow me to chase my dream.

To my daughters, Armani, Imani and Khadija, for always believing in me. To my mother, who taught me the meaning of sacrifice. Dorothy Mullins, I love you dearly. To my father and Karen, who have always shown me what true determination is.

CHAPTER ONE

The door slams shut. *Wham!* And the force of the door sends chills down her spine. Tara closes her eyes. That's all she can do. She has absolutely no control now. As if the slamming of the bathroom door isn't enough, she hears the lock turn. *Click.* Shutting her out of the room that she is so close to, yet feels so far away from.

"Lord, please!" she prays. "Please don't let him kill my son."

Wh-tsh!

With the first crack of the belt, she gasps for air, ears glued to the wooden door.

"Didn't I!"

Wh-tsh!

"Tell you to…"

Wh-tsh! Wh-tsh! Wh-tsh! Wh-tsh!

Tears stream down her cheeks, her head shaking with disbelief.

Wh-tsh! Wh-tsh! Wh-tsh!

The sporadic cries of pain escaping her son's mouth weaken her body. She clings to the door as if it's holding her up. *What have I done? I should do something. I'm his mother.*

Wh-tsh! Wh-tsh!

Tara's heart drops. She clenches her fingers into a fist.

Wh-tsh! Wh-tsh! Wh-tsh! Wh-tsh!

"Stop moving!" he yells with a deep growl.

Wh-tsh!

There is a change in the young boy's cry. Before, Tara could count on a yelp after each slash. Now there is only the hiss of the belt whipping through the air, across his skin, the shallow breaths seeping from his tiny lungs, no screams, just air. She waits and prays. She holds on to his last cry. It is her only proof that he is still alive.

Wh-tsh! Wh-tsh!

"Thomas, stop!" Tara screams, banging on the door as if it'll budge.

"Stop!" Panic takes over. She drops, knees crashing to the white tiled floor. She crouches down, clasps her hands together and prays, "Stop him. Please stop him."

Wh-tsh!

Tara presses her fingers into her temples, rubbing off the sharp pain in her head. Just the thought of the kindness and the joys of childhood being stripped from her son and being replaced with hate, anger, and resentment force more tears to trickle down her face. She knows all too well the everlasting affects of being beaten until you give up, beaten until you conform to whatever it is your mother, father or "man" wants you to become.

"Now, I bet you won't do it again!" Thomas warns one last time as he lands the last whip across David's back.

Tara hears a loud thump inside the bathroom, her son's body dropping to the floor. She gasps, her body rigid and stricken with fear.

Suddenly, she too falls into the bathroom as Thomas yanks the door open. She glances up at his broad shoulders and thick build. He is hovering over her trembling body. "What are you looking at?" he says. He stares at her, until her eyes fall to the cold bathroom floor. He steps over her, making sure his foot bumps into her shoulder.

Tara watches him grab a glass of lemonade out of the refrigerator, lie down on the couch in the living room, prop his legs on the ottoman and form a sick smirk. The only thing missing in Thomas's world is the jewel encrusted crown and beautiful half-naked women around him dangling fresh grapes over his lips.

As she stares at him, more chills surge through her body. She doesn't know if it's from the sudden draft sweeping cold air through the house or from the hate she feels toward him. She crawls to her son. David's legs are stretched across the floor, head resting on the blue rug that's nestled in front of the toilet. She lifts his head and examines his body. He is naked with only a damp, brown bath towel covering his thigh. Droplets of soapy water and sweat cover him, his tiny chest jumps, his lungs struggling to return to their natural rhythm.

Tara holds him while her eyes scan his body. They stop at the emerging bruises and blood that has oozed its way to the surface. "I'm so sorry, baby. I'm so sorry," she chants, sniffing and wiping tears from her face. She rocks him back and forth.

David tries to nestle in his mother's arms, but it only brings more agony. His teeth clench down on his bottom lip, but it's no match to the pain that's throbbing along his lower back, his thighs, arms, and legs. Staring at the wall, he imagines himself bigger, older and able to fight back. He dreams of the day his mother gets a job, packs up her bags and leaves his father. That was her promise to him, her excuse she gave him years ago, the reasons why she can't leave just yet. In his dream, she is smiling because she can finally live on her own. It's these thoughts, these bursts of hope that help him to endure such violent whippings. Slowly, his mind eases back into reality. He opens his mouth and struggles to force out the words with each hiccuping breath. "Ma-mee, I di-dn't break it."

"Shh. I know, baby. I know." Wishing that somehow the whole incident could be undone, Tara rocks David, and replays the incident in her head:

It was mid-afternoon. The air conditioning had just kicked in, startling Tara and reminding her to check the time. When she glanced at the ticking hands and read the clock, her heart sped up.

"Dammit. I forgot. It's Tuesday," she said, "Thomas comes home early today." Snatching the broom from the corner of the kitchen, she scrambled to sweep the floor. As she swept, she'd use her free hand to fluff the brown couch pillows, use her knee to align the end tables and examined the room for anything out of place. She quickly brushed the last bits of trash into a pile, making sure not to leave even a crumb behind.

But as Tara bent down to grab the dust pan, the broom slipped out of her hand. A rush of air passed her head, followed by a crash. She jumped back. "Shit!" At first she was relieved that it didn't smack her in the head, but when her eyes caught a glimpse of the shattered trophy, she covered her mouth and whispered, "Oh no!" Seeing Thomas's only trophy clumped up in pieces in the midst of dirt and dust, her body stiffened. "He is going to kill me!"

She sat pieces of it up, trying to measure the damage. The tube of superglue was in one hand and two of the biggest broken pieces in the other. She shook her head at the two fragments of glass. There was no saving it. She placed the pieces back on the mantle and yelled for David to get in the tub. Singing to herself to calm her nerves, Tara wished that Thomas's anger management class – the one mandated by the courts – would help her. She sang the words to a gospel hymn from her childhood. "Glory, glory, hallelujah…" She hummed and silently prayed.

Within minutes, Thomas's footsteps stopped at the front door, the keys clashed against the metal knob, causing her breaths to shorten. She clenched her jaw while twisting the soapy cloth around in the glass cup, praying he wouldn't see the broken trophy, hoping he was in a good mood. She wrestled with her thoughts. *Maybe I should have hid it. No, he would have noticed it being gone anyway. I should have been more careful. I know better.*

She followed the sound of his heavy footsteps around the living room and when they paused, she took in a deep breath. "What the fuck?" she heard him say.

Squeezing her eyes like a child blocking out the anticipation of a scary monster, a boogeyman popping up from thin air, her thoughts ran wild. The fear in her heart was real; she'd thought the worst and it came true. The boogeyman, the scary monster, had just stepped right in the doorway of the kitchen, breathing deeply and waiting for an explanation.

"What happened to my shit?" Thomas yelled. He stood there holding a piece of the molded glass.

Tara didn't look up. Her eyes stayed fixed on the suds that were popping and the dirty cups that were bobbing up and down in the dish water.

"David, he...uh. He was bouncing the basketball," she stuttered.

Thomas didn't allow her to finish. He turned from the kitchen and stomped through the hallway to find David.

"David!" he yelled, first opening the boy's bedroom door. "Daaavid," he said as if playing a game of Hide and Go Seek.

Still in the kitchen, washing and rinsing the dishes, Tara listened while Thomas opened and closed doors. Her heart sped up as she waited.

"Yes, Dad?" David said, so childlike, so ignorant of the situation.

Tara tiptoed to the hallway with suds still running down her hand. She could see Thomas hold up the broken pieces and give David a piercing stare. She stood there, silent, as David lowered his head to his chest. Not a word came from his mouth. He fiddled around the water for his cloth and waited. *I've got to tell him the truth. I can't.* Tara put her head down and walked back to the kitchen.

Tara looks down at the marks spread across her son's body. It takes her mind back to the movie *Roots.* The similarities blow her mind. Images of Kunte Kinte being stripped down to his bare skin and being ruthlessly whipped until his will breaks engulfs her sanity. It brings chills to her body, makes her stomach nauseous and her heart pound. She can only think of one difference. Instead of being whipped by his master, her son was lifted up with one hand, his legs fighting the air, by a man that looks much like him - his father. It's a scene that she is all too familiar with, even as a child herself.

"I'm sorry, baby," Tara whispers, wishing that those words could lighten the load of guilt her heart carries. She wipes the tears from her cheek and licks the salty residue from her lips. "We are going to get out of here. I promise. We are going to get out of here," and with a soft touch, she smoothes her fingers along her son's arm to calm him.

A shallow knock against the glass portion of the screen door echoes through the house.

"Can David come out?" Daniel, the neighbor's kid, yells through the screen. Thomas eyes the little boy who is bending the flimsy screen with his head as he leans in to get a closer look inside.

"No, he cannot!" Thomas yells back. "And get off my damn screen."

"What's wrong, Daniel?" his mother asks.

"David can't come out. He never gets to come out," Daniel says.

"Well, maybe he's busy."

Sheri glances at her son, who is still dressed in his school clothes – a crisp blue button down, khakis, and a pair of brand new loafers. She forces a weak frown. "Maybe I'll go over there tomorrow and see if he can ride with us to school."

Dressed in a knee length skirt with a flowered baking apron on, Sheri kneels down to her son and stretches out her arms. "Come here. Give your mother a nice big hug." She squeezes him tightly and then kisses him on his round forehead. "Mommy loves you."

"*Okay,* Mom," Daniel says, pulling away from her. "I'm not a damn baby."

"Well, you are my baby," she responds. "Come. Help me set the table."

Daniel rolls his eyes, but helps anyway. He carries the ceramic bowls filled with whipped garlic mashed potatoes, creamy gravy, and steaming green beans to the table. He then places each dish in its proper position and waits for his mother to bring out the rest.

Sheri pulls out the china and silverware, and as her husband walks through the front door, she is pulling the garlic bread out of the stainless steel oven. The aroma of herbs, butter and garlic fill the room.

"Sorry I'm late," her husband says in a hurry. "I'm starving."

The athletic man unbuttons his police jacket, revealing his bright white t-shirt and thick muscular arms, and slings it along the couch. He rubs his cold hands together and loosens his belt.

From the draping tablecloth to the freshly polished wooden chairs, everything is arranged as if they are expecting company. Even the utensils are set properly - perfectly aligned - allowing them to easily work from the outside in. As a family, they stretch their hands out while Jacob leads prayer. "Lord, thank you for the food. Amen." From the knives slicing through the ham and the forks trying to stay in position, but sliding across the plates, it sounds like a band of violins are in dire need of a tuning.

"I had to respond to a last minute call," Jacob says, passing the gravy bowl to Daniel. "A man was stoned, running around in and out of traffic, naked." He chuckles in disbelief. "And this was after he assaulted a woman in the thrift store - you know, the one just off of 123rd and Broadway."

Jacob pauses for a second to take a big bite out of his swollen honey dinner roll. "That damn crack," he says in the middle of a chew.

"Crack? What's crack?" Daniel asks. His eyes light up, his voice heightens.

"Nothing," Sheri blurts. "It's nothing for you to worry about."

Daniel sighs. "You never want to tell me anything," he mumbles.

"Crack is a substance that people ingest into their bodies to escape the real world," his father says, smiling at him. "It's a bad drug that will destroy your life. It not only affects the addict's life, but the community suffers, the kids with parents in jail suffer, the mothers who are on the corner selling their —"

Sheri interrupts. "Enough about work." She signals Jacob to hush while eyeing Daniel's fully focused and excited stare.

"So, how has your day been going, honey?" Jacob asks.

"Great! Today I met with Daniel's teacher. I wish you could have been there. His teacher talked so highly of him. He is especially doing well in science and is sure to move on to middle school. Our son is going to be a doctor one day, right Daniel?" She glances at him in admiration.

"Right."

After dinner, Sheri tells Daniel to take a shower, and then, as if he is still a toddler, she reads him a bedtime story. She tucks him in and gives him yet another kiss on his forehead.

"Goodnight, Sweetie."

She flips off the light switch and smiles back at her son whose face is glowing from the baseball lamp positioned next to his bed.

"Jacob, I don't know about our neighbors," Sheri says while lying down next to her husband in her flowered silk kimono. "I think something is going on with that poor little boy."

"What neighbors? What boy?"

"The ones that just moved next door. You know, the ones on Section 8."

Jacob nods. "Okay?" he says sarcastically.

"Their son always looks sad. He is never allowed to come out of the house. I don't think they like us very much," Sheri adds.

"Well, they are probably keeping to themselves," Jacob says, adjusting his pillow behind his head.

Sheri twists her lips like she just bit into a lemon. "I don't know about that, dear," she says, rubbing her fingers along Jacob's chest hair. "I'm telling you, the way they dress him, as if they don't own a washer and a dryer, they should be grateful he has a clean cut friend like our Daniel. He could be a great role model, you know." She stops to imagine her son helping the raggedy looking boy straighten up his image. She smiles at her brilliant idea. "You know what? We have some leftover ham in the refrigerator. I should have Daniel—"

Suddenly, a loud ring echoes throughout the house. It's the phone. Jacob slings the covers from his waist and jumps out of bed. Sheri crawls out of bed, tiptoes to the doorway, and stretches out her neck as far as possible to hear every word that comes tumbling out of Jacob's mouth.

"Hello? Hi, Dad!" Jacob says to his father on the phone. He leans on the refrigerator, taking shallow breaths to slow down his breathing.

"No. I told you his birthday is on the 14th, not the 7th," Jacob explains. "It's *next* weekend."

Jacob shakes his head.

"Oh! I knew that!" Jacob's father says so loudly through the phone, the neighbors could probably hear him. "I haven't been feeling well lately. I was really calling to let you know that I am unable to make it to see him for his birthday. What are your plans?"

Jacob rests his forehead on the counter and takes in another deep breath. He controls his tone to hide his irritation. "Oh, nothing big, just a small get-together."

His father quickly chimes in. "Listen, I will deposit some money into Daniel's account sometime tomorrow." Jacob lifts his head from the counter so fast his head starts spinning. "So get whatever you need, all right?"

"Dad, why do you always insist on paying for things?" Jacob tries to stop the big smile from affecting his voice. "The go-kart, the big screen TV, hell, everyone in the neighborhood is going to think we're rich."

His father lets out a laugh, but a series of dry coughs interrupt it. "That never stops you from going to the bank, son, now does it?" He pauses to cough again. "Just get the boy something nice. I feel terrible that I can't make it."

After hanging up the phone with his father, Jacob's breaths settle. His heart immediately thumps with anticipation. He nervously combs his fingers through his black stringy hair, and while nodding his head, he ponders for a second, *I wonder if Sheri heard him.* He softly snaps his fingers. *I should have gone down to the basement.*

Jacob eases his way back into the bedroom and walks straight into their bathroom; he can feel Sheri's eyes following him every step of the way. His body tenses up, his heart speeds up, but he is trying to act normal. Not too excited, but not too relaxed. He's anticipating at least three grand. He bites down on the smile that's forming. *I'll have enough to throw Jacob a nice party. That will get Sheri off my back. And have a little bit left over for…"*

Tara smacks the jumping alarm clock on her nightstand, trying to deaden its tired and worn out sound. "Damn, it's too early in the morning for this shit," she complains. She forces the thick comforter back over her head. She lies there on a bed of Thomas's curly chest hair and tightens her squeeze around him. *He is going to change. I know it,* she thinks.

Her mind takes her back to the wild night they shared just before the sun went down. Images of Thomas's strong hold around her waist as he moaned and groaned, the strength he used to pull her body every which way he wanted to, pulling her hair back and the sweet whispers in her ears are flashing through her mind. Goosebumps are forming, growing on her arms just thinking about it. It puts a smile on her face. "I know he loves me," she whispers as she gets lost in her thoughts. She looks up at Thomas. He's sleeping so peacefully, barely even making a sound. A bigger smile grows on her face.

The beaming sun peeking through the curtains remind her of the time. Tired, exhausted, and even sore in some areas of her body, she drags herself to her feet. She glances at the two tall bottles of Belvedere and the stack of unopened bills beside them. *What am I going to do if he can't find another job? I'm not moving back to the Projects. I don't care what I have to do.* She takes in a deep breath and shakes her head. *Why does my life have to be so damn hard?*

"Wake up, D! Wake up!"

Tara slings the covers from David's bruised body and smacks him on his butt. He doesn't move, so she whacks him again. With his eyes still closed, David just lies there. The first hit had woken him up, but he continues to lie there to get a few more minutes of sleep.

"You better not miss that bus," Tara says, trying to clear the sleep from her voice.

David gradually opens one eye. *Whack.* She hits him again.

"Okay. I'm up," he says, jumping down from the wooden bunk bed.

"Make sure you wear long sleeves, you hear."

"Yes, ma'am."

CHAPTER TWO

The screeching brakes of the bus lets David know time is slipping away. Gliding his hand across the smooth wooden bottom, he pushes socks and underwear to the side, but no sign of a long sleeve shirt. He tries slamming the drawer shut, but it won't close all the way. *I don't want to get another whipping,* he thinks. His heart beats faster and his stomach is turning to knots. He doesn't have time to spare. He yanks the wooden drawer all the way out and sticks his arm in the hole. He fiddles around carefully as to not gain a splinter from the raw wooden surface while feeling for the mysterious object. His fingers stop at something. He pulls it out and rubs its dusty plastic cover. It's a photo album.

David flips the first page. It's the only page with a picture. He brings the picture closer and tilts his head. It's a picture of a baby swaddled in a white blanket, a tall dark man holding it in his arms. A thick chain is hanging from the man's neck, bright gold rings on his fingers. Then there is his mother, a much younger Tara. She is standing beside him with the biggest smile David had ever seen.

"David!" Tara gasps. She slaps the album from David's hand and just as fast snatches it from the floor. Her piercing eyes and twisted face frighten David even more. He swallows deeply while staring back at her.

"The bus is here," she says.

Wearing just a pair of jeans, David jets outside and yanks a shirt from the clothes line. He's moving so fast that the cold air slams into his chest, making his jaw quiver.

As he darts back into the house, he remembers the last time he'd missed the bus and was hit upside the head with a drum stick. The memory makes him move faster. Quickly sliding his arms into his jacket, stuffing his feet into his shoes, and grabbing his book bag, he flies out of the front door. On his way out he sees Daniel and his mother, walking toward the porch.

"Hey, glad I was able to catch you. Is your mother at home?" David hears Daniel's mom ask.

"Yes, but she doesn't like company. I gotta go," David blurts out, darting past the two and running toward the closing doors of the bus. He reaches the bus just in time.

Out of breath, David finds a seat at the front of the bus and is relieved that he has just dodged another skin-tearing whipping. He stares out the foggy window, bringing back the memory of the picture he'd found. *Why was that picture in my drawer and who was that…*

"Ew, what is that smell?" a boy yells.

David's thoughts of the man holding the baby with his mother smiling so proudly disappear.

"Sit down, Maurice. Sit down," the bus driver commands.

"What is that smell?" the boy yells again in pure disgust, causing everyone to sniff their limbs in the hopes that it isn't them.

Every kid on the bus looks around and sniffs the air like little puppies in search of the mysterious stench.

"It smells like a dirty dog," one boy says, sitting two seats from David.

"No, it smells like an old dirty rag," the boy next to David blurts out.

David sniffs himself along with the other kids, but takes in nothing but the smell of his jean jacket.

"It's you, David," a boy sitting right behind him says. He points to the back of David's head.

David puts his head down. "Ugh," he says, jerking his head back up. *It is* me. "Mildew. I guess my mom put the clothes out on the line too late again."

He shakes his head. The whole bus is filled with laughter and nasty jokes are being thrown toward David, along with pointing fingers. The bus driver even covers his nose for a second. With all of the laughing and snickering, all David can do is look out the window and watch the houses get bigger, the yards become greener and the sun shine brighter the farther away he gets from his street; the street that separates the inner city, East Mount Projects from the suburbs, Garrison Heights.

"Two weeks living here and nothing has changed," David mumbles to himself. He looks through the smudged window and stares at the world passing by. He sits up in his seat, his eyes following the huge houses surrounded by thick green acres of grass, the exotic cars pulling from the driveway.

I wish I had money like them. If I had money I would be rockin' Jordans, wearing gold chains. My mom would be living in a big house just like that. My life would be perfect. I gotta get money. I don't care how. I'm gonna get it.

Walking home from the bus stop, David spots Daniel and his father jumping high on their trampoline. Their bodies are free to stretch out and jump as high as the strength in their legs will carry them. The beautiful blue sky is just out of their reach; clouds are floating above them like a batch of thick cotton candy.

His mind takes him to the last time he'd jumped on anything. It was an old stained mattress. Something someone had abandoned on the side of a dumpster. The thought of being the first to discover it, finding the strongest parts of the mattress and being able to jump above the stinky brown dumpster makes him smile. However, the fun never did last. Once the word got out that there was a mattress by the dumpster, all of the kids in East Mount Projects would fight and push to get a turn.

He stretches his neck out and tries to see over the tall wooden fence. "I wonder if they can touch the sky," he says. He remembers the mattress that was filled with metal springs bursting from the seams and stitching. "No matter how high I tried to jump, I could never get past the top of the dumpster. But I bet they can."

"Hey, David!" a man yells.

David turns around and sees Daniel's father open the wooden fence and walk toward him. He's out of breath, but still able to speak clearly.

"You know, if you ever want to come over and play ball or," Jacob points to Daniel, who is still gliding in the air, "jump on the trampoline, you are more than welcome."

David nods his head, trying to hide his excitement when Sheri comes speeding toward them.

"Jacob, your father is on the phone."

Jacob takes the cordless from Sheri and walks to the side of the house.

David stands there pondering whether or not he could get a couple of jumps in before his father notices his absence. He slings his book bag against the fence, climbs halfway up the trampoline, but before he is even able to gather his balance, Jacob comes back over.

"Listen," Jacob says. "I have to go to the bank. I'll be right back."

"Ooh. Can I go?" Daniel blurts.

David jumps down from the trampoline, feeling half disappointed and half relieved that he didn't get caught jumping by his father. He grabs the arm of his book bag, waves goodbye to Daniel, and then walks across the lawn to his house.

"Ooh. I want to go," Daniel begs, jumping as high as he can in the air and then landing on the grass. "Ooh. Ooh. Can I?" He wraps his arms around his father's waist. "Pa-lease!"

"No, not this time," Jacob says.

"You okay, honey?" Sheri asks.

"Yep. Everything is just fine."

"Can I go, please!" Daniel asks again.

"*Sure*," Jacob says.

Jacob rushes Daniel into the car. He speeds to the bank and withdraws the thirty-five hundred dollars his father deposited. He circles around the block a couple of times, driving nervously and then stops at a house.

"Wait in the car, I'll only be a minute," he says to Daniel.

Daniel pushes down on the door locks as instructed. Ducked down in the backseat, he is punching the buttons on his Game Boy and swaying the tiny system in his hand as if it will motivate Mario to jump higher, run faster. From time to time he looks up at the house to see if his father is coming, but there is no sign of him, just men coming in and out of the house.

After his last man gets struck by an axe, he checks to see if his father is coming. He still doesn't see him. His eyes, however, catch something else. Through the sheer curtains, he notices a girl. She is staring at the descending sun from her window. Squinting his eyes, he tries to focus in on her more, but it is to no avail. He gives up and starts a new game.

After a while, he sees his father running to the car. He looks down at his Game Boy to pause it and before he can look back up again, his father is tapping at the door for him to unlock it. *I hope he doesn't get mad because I wasn't paying attention.*

It is something that his father taught him a couple of years ago, to always unlock the door *before* he makes it to the car. During trips like this, he is usually on point, lifting the knob from the door right on time, but this time he fell short.

Daniel looks at his father, who is sweating bullets and huffing for air, and says, "Dad, that didn't take long."

Without swaying his eyes from the road, Jacob hesitates, and then says, "I know. I am in a bit of a hurry. Just make sure we keep this between me and you, son."

"Always, Dad," Daniel says with a proud smile.

CHAPTER THREE

"*What am I going to say?*" David thinks while watching his classmates proudly proclaim what they want to be when they grow up.

He imagines his father walking into the door reciting Notorious B.I.G, "It was all a dream, I used to read Word Up Magazine…" His heart races with excitement. Biggie's deep voice gets him to bopping his head, making him feel confident. He's pumped, ready to be called on next. "I can be a rapper!"

His teacher, Ms. Terrell, a young blonde woman whose layered hair bounces at every move, skims the room of flapping hands and dancing fingers. She points to another student. "Tyler, you are next."

The short and chubby boy jumps out of his seat and marches up to the front of the class like the general of an army. He is dressed simply, wearing a long sleeve dress shirt, blue khaki pants along with a striped bow tie. "I am going to be a lawyer," he projects to the class. "I am going to be a lawyer just like my father and my grandpa."

David watches the confident boy walk proudly to his seat. He becomes nervous. "A lawyer?" he mumbles while looking at other students as they run up to the front.

David stops tapping his pencil against the desk and hits his head with the palm of his hand. *I can't say that I want to be a rapper like my father. He's not a rapper. He doesn't have the chains, the cars, or even the girls.*

21

He runs through the names of people he'd looked up to in his life. *Who else can I be like?*

"Sam, it's your turn," Ms. Terrell says, breaking David's train of thought.

David immediately turns his head to the girl he has liked ever since his first day of school. His eyes widen at her caramel brown skin and stop at her long wavy black hair that remind him of his mother's soft curls after she gets out of the shower.

Sam walks with one foot in front of the other like a runway model from Paris. She looks at the class with slanted eyes she inherited from her Asian grandmother and stands tall.

"I want to become a fashion designer," she says. She twists her pink and white polka dot dress to control her nerves.

"Beautiful," the teacher says with her legs crossed and her body leaning toward Sam. "Now why do you want to become a fashion designer?"

Sam looks at her teacher's smile. "Because...my mother..." She pauses and looks at the dusty chalkboard, then turns to a laminated multiplication poster. Her head droops down as she smooths her hand over the lace on her dress. "Because my mother was a fashion designer."

"I understand," Ms. Terrell says, her voice filled with sympathy.

David watches Sam walk quietly back to her seat, studying every feature of her peculiar face.

"David!" the teacher says, interrupting his focus. "You are next."

David slides deeper into his hard wooden chair, pulls his hood over his head, and wishes he could disappear.

"David," Ms. Terrell repeats. "We don't have all day."

What am I going to say? he chants in his mind. He sits up slowly and then eventually stands up from the chair. Looking nervously around at all of the eyes focusing on him, he tries desperately to search for a career he might want to have. Inching his way to the front of the class, he thinks again, trying to conjure up a thought - any thought. He gets to the front row with the students kicking their legs up in the air and back down to their desk. *Oh... I know!*

"I got it!" he says.

"I'm glad you have it, David," Ms. Terrell says.

Mimicking his confident and bold classmates, David stands tall and stretches his neck out to add an inch or two to his height.

"I want to be a garbage man!" he says.

"Ha! Ha!" The room fills with a laughing roar. Some kids are chanting, "Garbageman, garbageman, dirrrty ol' garbageman," while the others are laughing out of control. One boy even blurts out, "You sure smell like one!"

David immediately glances at Sam's face. She is the only kid not laughing. Instead, her eyes are reassuring to him, her smile genuine. His eyes wander down to the blue and white checkered floor. Standing there confused, he is afraid to move a muscle.

"Class, be quiet!" Ms. Terrell says. "Why do you want to be a garbage collector, David?" she says with a softer tone of voice.

David starts to mumble. "Well, I... I see the men picking up our trash; they get to jump on the side of that big truck and ride through the neighborhood. They always smile and wave at me." He lifts his head up high again. "Plus... my father says they make a lot of money!"

The class busts out into laughs again; it's an orchestra of high and low levels of laughter. Totally depleted, David lowers his head and his shoulders follow. He walks back to his seat and wishes that his life was more like the other kids - the kids who had money, big houses, nice shiny cars and parents who were lawyers.

"Class, line up. It's time for dismissal," Ms. Terrell says.

David is the first to jump out of his chair. He races to the line to get a spot right behind Sam. He steps up a little bit closer to tighten the gap. However, the closer he gets to her, the further her little Mary Jane shoes inch away from him.

"Sam," he whispers. He has been wanting to call her name all morning, but was too nervous. "Sam."

She doesn't turn her head.

With a heavy and rapid-beating heart, David steps back. He steps back until he feels his heels rise up on someone's toes.

"Ouch!" the girl behind him yells out.

"Oops. I'm sorry," he says nervously.

David swings his book bag to his other arm.

Sam looks back at him and smiles.

Maybe she do like me, David thinks. David's heart pounds as he smiles back at her. *I wish she was my girlfriend.* He wiggles his toes through a small hole in his Nikes - the ones his mother found hidden under a rack of shirts at the thrift store for six dollars, and he rubs the dark blue patch sewn on the knees of his jeans.

He scans the room, his new reality of a class full of the privileged. *That won't happen. Girls like boys with cars and money.*

Heading home from school, David spots Sam. She is walking alone, her bright pink book bag bouncing with every stride.

David hesitates. Then he smiles. He speeds up his pace and gets within a couple of feet from her. His heart is beating fast and his mind is giving him every reason why he should not talk to her. *She doesn't like you. You stink.* The closer he gets to her, the louder the voices become. But David refuses to listen.

"You're it," he says, tugging at her back strap hanging from her book bag.

Sam turns around with a bright smile.

"Nuh uh. You're it," Sam says, taking off running.

She runs past a couple of trees, her ponytail bouncing up and down and all around. She ducks behind a wooden bench and bends down to catch her breath. She stands up at the sound of a crackling branch, the sound getting closer and closer. She pokes her head out just a tad. "Got-cha!" she says, poking David's shoulder.

David falls to the ground laughing, arms stretched out on the grass, sun beaming down on him.

Sam stoops down and giggles. "David. You are funny."

"Who, me?" David says, pointing to his poked out chest.

"Yes. You are stinky, but funny."

David frowns for a second, but then cracks a smile. *She is so pretty*, he thinks studying her smile and soft giggle. Sam extends her hand out to David, pulling him to his feet.

"Are you going to walk me home?" Sam asks.

David's face lights up. "Sure!" He slightly hunches his back; his stride loosens. He deepens his voice as much as he can. "You see. Where I come from. It's dangerous. My mother told me that girls shouldn't walk alone."

Sam nods her head and tightly grips her book bag straps. "So where did you move from?"

"East Mount," David says proudly.

Sam jerks her head back surprised. "My stepmother said that East Mount was bad. And that I should never go down the hill because I might get shot."

David laughs. "It's not even that bad. I mean..." He shakes his head to gather his thoughts, but can't seem to catch them. "I don't know. Sometimes it can get bad, but most of the time it's fun. We have block parties, we have cookouts. It's like a big family."

"Really?"

"Yep." David nods his head with a smile.

"This is my house," Sam says, stepping in the middle of her cracked driveway.

"I guess I'll see you tomorrow then."

Sam knocks on the door for a second. All the while David is standing there tapping his shoes on the concrete. He watches her walk onto her front porch, step back down, and then walk to the side door.

He takes in a deep breath. *Yeah. I think she can be my friend.*

Once Sam disappears into her house, David turns around and almost bumps into three men walking swiftly by him. They look suspicious. He watches them walk right up Sam's driveway and enter through her front door.

David's mind automatically goes back to his experiences in East Mount. How the neighborhood kids would mark certain houses and name them according to the people that traveled in and out.

"What's up with that?" he whispers. The men make him nervous. However, he will never forget the golden rule he learned from the Projects: "Mind your own business."

CHAPTER FOUR

"**D**avid, is that you?" Thomas yells from the dark living room with only a light reflecting from the television.

"Yes," he mumbles.

"David. Walk to the store and get me a shell."

David rolls his eyes thinking about the long walk down the hill to East Mount.

"I'll let you keep a quarter," Thomas says.

David's eyes widen. His heart jumps fast thinking about that shiny piece of metal. The last time he held a quarter in his hand was when he was living in East Mount and he stole a quarter from his mother's laundry jar. He shakes his head. He remembers so vividly the whipping, but he also remembers how juicy the frozen block of ice was that he bought with the quarter from the candy lady living upstairs; its bright red color and its sweet Kool-aid taste flipped over in a Styrofoam cup.

With the money in his hand, David walks down to East Mount, just a couple of streets down the hill to go to the corner store. It's the nearest store that will allow him to buy the cigar shell he needs and that also sells candy by the nickel.

Once he passes his street, the homes magically shrink, the green grass fades, and the trash on the street appears out of nowhere. It is nothing to David. Just a couple of weeks ago, that same environment was his home.

David stops at the first traffic light. At first he stares at his old school, a building that has since been boarded up and plastered with illegal art work. Its colors are beaming off of the building, but are mostly hidden from the tall weeds and vines slithering up its structure. Then he spots something else. It pulls up right in front of him. Adrenaline rushes through his body.

Waiting in front of the traffic light is a shiny silver Porsche 911. David stares at the car so long, he misses his turn to cross. He listens to the Porsche as it takes off, engine roaring and smoke pulling away from the tires. He closes his eyes. For a second, he takes himself back to a couple of years ago when he first laid eyes on the car of his dreams.

Dressed in cotton Spiderman pajamas, dragging a toy car along the walls of the tiny apartment, David heard a loud engine. The sound was so rough, yet so sweet, he stopped his toy car in mid-air to see where the sound was coming from. It came from the TV. The movie *No Man's Land* was playing. He looked at Charlie Sheen speed through the streets and immediately fell in love.

Vroom, vroom, vroom.

David rose up at the sound of the engine, standing only inches from the TV. "What kind of car is that?" he asked his father, who was lying down on the couch.

"Oh, that car?" his father said.

David caught the glisten in his father's eyes, the rare sense of admiration for something.

"That's a Porsche 911, the baddest car ever made."

His father's positive words shocked him. He had finally made his father smile.

With his toy car in his hand, standing up tall and proud, David said, "I'm going to get that car one day."

Thomas let out a boisterous laugh.

"Don't hold your breath, son. You'll never be able to get one." Thomas let out another series of laughs. "You better think about getting a damn job."

Just as quickly as the thought entered David's mind, his dreams were crushed; burning desire smothered by a thick blanket of impossibility. David crouched back down to the floor and continued imagining himself in the driver seat of his toy cars.

The cars that he zoomed in the air and crashed into each other were solid-colored toy cars, not Hotwheels - miniature replicas of the real thing. However, it didn't stop him from imagining himself behind the wheels, feeling the engine up under him and being free to speed far away from home.

David crosses the street and walks through the corner store parking lot. He is stopped by a man with a toothless smile and bulging gums.

"Do you have change?" the man asks David.

David walks right by him, immune to the poverty stricken streets.

Looking up at Nick's Food Mart, nothing much has changed. It is still covered with liquor posters and W.I.C. and food stamp signs. Even the lottery sign with the removable jackpot numbers is still hanging and flashing its lights, tempting people to spend their last dollar on a hope and a dream.

David jumps onto the curb as a car pulls into the parking lot. His heart speeds up at the sound of the banging music coming from the car and the beauty of the shiny chrome wheels. He mouths the words to the song, "All eyes on me," nods his head and follows the cleanest Bimmer he has ever seen.

David stands there in awe, waiting to see who's driving such an expensive car. The first thing that appears from under the opened car door is a pair of red and black patent leather Air Jordan's - the latest that dropped. He then sees a tall, dark-skinned man with a thick gold chain weighing down on his neck and glistening diamond earrings in his ears as he stands up. His black hair is freshly faded and he's wearing a white t-shirt along with a pair of Enyce jeans. Then another person gets out. It's a beautiful young girl in her twenties. So beautiful, in fact, that while David's jaw is stuck open, he doesn't even realize that the man, known as KG, is giving him a cold stare.

"You looking at my girl?" KG says, standing tall and intimidating.

David grips his book bag for security.

"Naw, I was…uh," he stutters.

KG laughs.

"I'm just playing, little man. What's your name?"

David looks up at the man in such admiration, you would have thought the president was standing there. "Um. David."

"David, huh? Where you live?"

David's eyes roll to the sky as if the answer is written in the clouds. He pauses, takes a deep breath and then says, "I live on East Overlook."

"Oh. You live up in Garrison Heights, huh. Whachu doin' down here?"

"Um. I wanted to buy some candy." He waits for the man to respond, but he doesn't. Instead, KG nods his head, glancing at David's faded jeans, his dangling book bag strap and stops at his uncombed hair. His hard expression loosens. David looks away.

"Li'l man, come on," KG says, waving his hand.

For a second David is stuck. The diamonds sparkling from KG's hands are mesmerizing, unbelievable to him. He shrugs his shoulders and then catches the door. He follows the man inside the store, catching a whiff of his masculine, yet pleasant cologne, but not before looking back at the Bimmer. It is still running. It's still gyrating in the parking lot and even though the music is muffled, he can still feel the beat to the song under his feet.

What man leaves his car running in the hood?

Walking behind KG is a different experience for David. As the store's alarm chimes, David picks up on how grown men - men that David assumed to be tough - move out of their way like KG is parting the Red Sea. While walking down the chips aisle, his eyes follow a man who hurries the other way, dodging any contact with KG.

"Whats up, KG?" a tall man says, staring at a bag of Lays potato chips. He never looks up. Instead, he only tightens his grip on the thick yellow bag, eyes focused, face serious, acting like he's interested in his calorie intake.

KG nods his head and continues through the store.

The young girl grabs a bag of pork rinds and a pink lemonade Snapple.

"What was you tryna get?" KG asks David.

"I was going to buy some…," his head tilts up to the ceiling, "Now-N-Laters."

"Go 'head and grab 'em. Matter of fact, take whatever you want."

A big smile covers David's face as he runs from aisle to aisle searching for the snacks he's always wanted. He's in Candyland and everything is free. Suddenly the store seems brighter. His senses have taken over looking at all of the colorful candies and bottles of soda of all shapes and sizes and the many flavors of chips that are bursting with air.

First, David grabs a coke. Then with his other hand, he takes a bag of Ranch Doritos and stuffs it in the pit of his arm. He goes to the next aisle. There are so many colorful boxes of candy displayed that the Now-N-Laters don't look that appealing anymore. He grabs some Boston

Beans and Lemon Heads and lodges them in between the chips and his arm.

With everything in hand, he stands really close to KG.

"That's all, little man? That's all you want?"

"Yep," David says, cheesing as if he is posing for a school picture.

"Seven dollars and twenty-seven cents," the cashier says.

KG pulls out a thick wad of money. With it comes a strong smell of freshly printed bills. The folded dough is so large he can barely hold it in place with one hand. He pulls off the rubber band, flips through a number of hundred dollar bills and then pulls out a twenty.

David's heart beat speeds up. "Whoa."

David has never seen so much money before. Even his mother's colorful book of food stamps is no match for the stack of bills his eyes are witnessing. Matter of fact, the only money he ever sees are from the large amounts of money stuffed in suitcases on gangster movies he watches with his father. His eyes open wider. It is surreal. *People really get money like that?*

After accepting the change, KG signals for David to move to the side. He looks down at him and says, "If you can count it, you can keep it."

KG raises an eyebrow. He waits for a smile to spread over David's face, a smirk, something, but it never forms. Instead, he is given a nervous stare.

"Go 'head and count it," KG commands.

David pulls the one dollar bill from KG's hand and says, "One dollar." He pulls another bill and says "two," but when he pulls the five dollar bill, he gets confused, loses his confidence and turns away from the money.

KG bites his lip. His eyes narrow at David. "Boy, you can't count?"

"Not money," David mumbles.

The Puerto Rican girl looks at KG and shakes her head. KG points to the car, and the half-naked girl does as she is told, quickly leaving them alone.

"Li'l man. Read this."

KG grabs a flyer off the magazine rack. David stares at the words.

"B-ad Cah-cah-ri…Cah," he says.

Instead of words, David sees the letters jumbling together like a bowl of alphabet soup.

"Bad credit approved," KG reads.

KG kneels down. He swings his arm around David, almost scooping his little body up.

"Listen here, you have to start paying attention in school. You have to learn how to read. Raise your damn hands and ask questions." KG looks around, as if he is trying to make someone an example. "Don't become one of these dumb motha…I mean, ignorant people out here. If I give you this money, you better learn how to count it." He stares at David. His eyes are so piercing that David is itching to turn away. "You better try to read any and everything you can. Ya heard me?"

David nods. It is the first time he had been pushed by someone other than his teacher back when he lived in East Mount. It is a feeling of joy mixed with embarrassment mixed with a determination to somehow make KG proud. He doesn't even know the man. But there is something about him - about the way he walks and talks - that gives David a sense of confidence.

KG slaps the bills in the palm of David's hand.

"Don't let nobody take your money either," he says before turning and walking away.

"You know what?" KG turns back around to say.

"Li'l D. Imma have my li'l sis holla at you. Give me your number and over the summer, she gon' teach you some shit. Aight?"

David stands in front of the store, clutching his paper bag and focuses in on KG's shining rims as the car pulls away. He closes his eyes. *I want to be just like KG. I don't care what I have to do. I want what he got. Money. Pretty girls.* He smiles. *Like Sam. And I want people to move when I walk past them.*

Pulling into the parking lot, just as David is remembering that he has to go back inside of the store to get what his father wanted, he sees a red rusty cavalier pull up. It's his mother, pissed as ever, driving her friend's car. David immediately gets so nervous he suddenly has to use the bathroom. *What am I going to say?*

Before Tara even puts the car into park, she's already yelling through the window. "What are you doing with all that junk in your hand? Didn't your father send you to the store to get some damn cigarettes? What's that?"

Tara parks the car, jumps out and snatches the bag of chips and candy out of his hands. "You got some nerve," she says, pulling David by his collar back into the store.

"You better be glad that man told me you didn't steal those chips," Tara says, while driving the car down the street.

As she talks, David just keeps looking out the window. He's grateful that the cashier didn't say anything about the money KG gave him.

"David, I know things are a little hard right now." Tara looks at her son's sad face. "But I promise you things are going to get better. Your father has a huge interview tomorrow. If he gets this job, then we won't have to move again," she says.

David blocks her words out. All he can think about is KG and how he could grow up to be like him. Unlike the shallow words and broken promises that are coming from his mother's mouth, what he saw in KG's hand in the store was real.

CHAPTER FIVE

"David!" Sam snaps her fingers around his head. "David. What are you thinking about?" she asks walking from the dismissal line. "Are you walking me home today?"

"Sure. Yeah," David says.

As they cross the street and David continues his silent stare, Sam stops and looks at him.

"What's wrong? Why are you so quiet?"

David stops and looks at Sam, his expression blank and still not saying a word.

"Sam. I just want to have money. Not be broke anymore. I want to move up the hill. I want to live on top of the hill. You know, I'm tired of not having what I want."

Sam nods her head and starts walking again. "I know."

Her words surprise David.

"You feel me? How can you feel me? You live closer to the hill than me. And I bet you don't have mean parents. You have a car and you always have the baddest clothes on." He looks at Sam's screwed up face as she smacks her lips.

"The clothes I wear, my mother made for me before she died. My father is dead, and I live with my crazy stepmother. *Some fairytale.*"

"But you are always happy," David says.

"My mother left me these journals," Sam says, shaking her head. "Well, I only have one for now. But in the journals she talks to me. She tells me that everything will be fine, if I just concentrate on the prize."

David stops walking and turns toward Sam. "So what's the prize?" he asks.

Sam shrugs her shoulders and starts walking again. "I don't know. I have to find the other journals. My stepmother, Courtney, won't give them to me, and I can't find them anywhere. One day I will find them."

Suddenly, David shouts, "I gotta go!"

"What's wrong?" Sam asks.

"My father has a interview today, and I have to be home."

David jets by Sam and is almost halfway down the street when she calls him back.

"David! I have something for you." She pulls out a crinkled piece of aluminum foil with something plump nestled inside.

David snatches it out of her hand. "Thanks, gotta go!"

Sam yells, "Happy Birthday!"

David smiles back at her and runs home.

Sam feels good that she is able to give David her piece of sweet cornbread from lunch. She smiles the rest of the way home, but once she makes it to her doorstep, she sighs.

Sitting at the kitchen table is Courtney, her stepmother, lighting up a wrinkled cigarette. The windows are covered with dingy yellow curtains, making it dark and dreadful inside. Sam can remember it being so beautiful in the room, but since her father died some years ago, she notices that it gets darker every year. From years of tar floating from Courtney's lungs into the air, the bright white paint has tanned, with dark brown spots sprinkled around the room.

"Let me see what you got here," Courtney says with a raspy voice.

Sam pulls out the noisy paper bag of canned chili, macaroni and cheese, and a variety of fruits that are swimming in thick syrupy juices, her free weekend lunch box. She remembers hearing the lunch lady complain about how much sodium companies put in off brand food and calling it a heart attack in a bag. She nods her head.

"Looks good for dinner. And you even have a granola bar," Courtney says with a slight smile.

Courtney tries to maintain a reassuring tone of voice. "We are going to have some food tomorrow. I promise." She raises Sam's head up to look deeply into her eyes. "Matter of fact, I'm going to take you to McDonald's." She points to the street. "You can get your favorite - a Big Mac, no pickles, extra sauce."

Sam cracks a smile, but she already knows what that means.

That means she will have to stay in her room all night. That means there will be a lot of people coming in and out of the house. There will be loud music, but unfortunately, not loud enough to mask the moaning and scary noises that come from the attic.

"Give me a kiss," Courtney says. She puckers her dark colored lips to Sam's cheek. "I love you so much, baby girl. This is only temporary. You've got your mother's word. Temporary, I say."

She holds her stepdaughter tightly. She tries to conceal the tears that are streaming down her face. "I know you miss your dad. I miss him, too," Courtney whispers.

Sam rises up from Courtney's arms and looks her straight into her eyes. "Can I have my other journals? My father said you would give them to me."

Knock. Knock.

The sound abruptly ends their conversation. Sam can feel the sudden trembling of Courtney's body.

"Oh. You gotta go now. Go to your room and remember that tomorrow I will take you to McDonald's," Courtney says in a rush.

Sam grabs the top of her bag and quickly heads upstairs. She locks her door behind her; the only door other than the front door with a padlock on it. Then she throws her headphones on and begins listening to Sam Cooke.

Sam Cooke is the only music that brings her closer to her father. He loved Sam Cooke and oldies that stirred the soul. Gazing out the window, Sam can see the city divided. On one side is abandoned buildings, zombie-like people moping the streets and police lights patrolling like it's Gotham City. And on the other side are blocks of big beautiful homes, tall oak trees lined up on every freshly cut lawn, and streets so quiet the birds' chirping echoes throughout the city. Sam shakes her head.

"I want to move farther up the hill, too, David," Sam whispers. "I want to move far, far, far away. All I have to do is find those journals."

Downstairs, Courtney opens the door to a tall man that is no stranger to her house. He grabs her by the arms and yanks her forward. Slightly used to the treatment, Courtney doesn't fight back.

"Hurry up. I ain't got all damn day," he says, pushing her backside up the steps to the attic.

CHAPTER SIX

"Thomas, I can't tell you how sorry I am," the hiring manager says.

The woman dressed in a caramel blouse with chocolate stones draping around her neck is wearing a fake, sympathetic smirk. Her eyes are bulging from her eye sockets as she tries to convince him of her genuine words.

Thomas just looks at her and then interrupts, "Okay, ma'am. Thank you for the opportunity."

He immediately stands up from the hard wooden chair and extends his hand out to her. The woman barely grips him as her fingers almost slip from his hand.

Once he leaves the tall building, with men and women rushing in and out of the doors going to a job that pays them to live without worries, he feels a sense of loss. *Damn. I ain't never gonna find a good job. How the hell am I supposed to make money when every interview I go to, they assume they know me just by reading a piece of paper? They won't even give me a chance. That was the past. I was only 16. And then the first thing they want to say is...*

He shakes his head to the rhythm of the words, "By checking this box it does not automatically disqualify you for the job." *Get the fuck out of here.*

The memory of him snatching the white eviction notice from the screen makes him even more upset. *I'm a felon. And I am always going to be a felon. It doesn't matter how I dress, talk or*

45

act. Once they look at that word "Felony," that's it. How am I supposed to feed my family?

"Tara. I ain't get the job," he says in the cramped phone booth. "What you think? Yeah. Just shut up." He slams the phone down on the metal hook.

Counting backwards and taking deep breaths, he does what his counselor says will help him.

After waiting an hour, Thomas finally boards the city bus. He easily finds a seat in the back and then a tear falls. "It's not easy coming from nothing. I don't care what people say," he says.

A graying woman beside him chimes in. "You are too young to think like that. Do you know what I had to go through when I was your age? Son, I couldn't even sit at the front of the bus without worrying about being dragged off like an animal, kicked, punched, spit on and thrown in jail."

Thomas narrows his eyes at the slow-talking woman as she continues.

"Y'all young folk don't know what struggle is. You think it's hard, but it's really not. Stop giving up so easily. Fight for what you want. All the pity in the world is not going to change your situation. Only you can," the woman says.

Thomas rolls his eyes and nods his head.

"Ten. Eleven. Twelve. Thirteen." David is sitting on the edge of his bed counting his money yet again. He pulls out a handful of change and lays the coins down on his blanket. Sliding each coin from one side to the other, he counts, "Twenty-five. Twenty-six. Twenty-seven." His eyes fill up with pride as he finally gets them all right. "I'm going to stack up my money like KG," David says.

But then the door swings open, interrupting his count. It's his mother.

"David!" she shouts. "What are you doing in here? I have been calling you and calling you. We have to hurry up and catch the bus so we can go to the store."

"Okay."

David stuffs the money in his back jean pocket and hurries to the living room where his mother is waiting.

"We have to go. Your dad just called and he wants dinner to be ready when he gets here. And we *still* have to go to the store."

"What got you so happy?" Tara says, watching David glide on the shopping cart through the cookie aisle.

"Nothing." David whips the cart around and rides back down the aisle. He uses his foot for brakes, allowing it to slide across the floor to slow down. Looking back at his mother, he smiles.

"Is it a *girl*. You're glowing," Tara says.

"*Mom*. I don't know what you're talking about."

"Sam, she got you all happy, don't she?" Tara says, joking around.

David watches his mother chuckle. He loves to see her show her pearly white teeth. It's such a rarity that when it graces her face, it warms him up inside. "Mom, do you think I can get a job?" David asks.

"A job? For what?"

"I don't know. I want a gold chain. I mean, some new shoes."

Tara looks at her son's shoes and then at his bright smile.

"What you *need* to do is stop watching all those music videos and concentrate on them books. They're polluting your little mind," she says, squeezing the top of his head. "You don't need anything. All that you need, you got, plus you're only ten. No one will hire you."

"What about if I start mowing grass?"

"We don't have a lawn mower," Tara snaps back.

"Umm, what about if I washed some cars?"

"Your father ain't gonna go for that."

Tara looks at David's smile morph into a sad, hopeless stare.

"Just wait, baby. Your time will come. Then you won't want to work."

"Like Daddy?" David says, wishing he could take the words back.

Tara cuts him a look and then jumps in line.

"Hello, Ma'am," the cashier says.

"Oh, hi."

Tara quickly stuffs the fashion magazine that was in her hand in front of a fitness magazine and immediately starts to pull items out of her basket and onto the conveyor belt. She never looks up at the red-haired cashier with braces shining brightly with spit. She is busy counting the cost of the items for the third time in her head.

As each item gets scanned and the register makes a beeping sound, Tara's heart beats faster.

"Twenty-five dollars and eighty-eight cents," the cashier finally says.

"Damn!" Tara blurts.

She looks over her bagged groceries wondering what caused such an offensive number. *Peanut butter, flour, drumsticks, chicken nuggets, potatoes…Oh, damn. The shrimp. I can't put the shrimp back. Thomas would kill me.*

With her food stamp book hidden in her purse, she thumbs through the colorful pages. In her head, she is counting away. *I know I had more stamps than this.*

From the corner of her eyes, Tara looks at the line of people who are now moaning and giving her impatient looks.

"Uh. Put back the peanut butter. I think I have some at home. And uh. The hamburger meat."

She watches the cashier scan the items and then pound button after button.

"Twenty dollars and fifty-two cents."

Satisfied with that, Tara digs deep inside her pocketbook for change. Her fingers swipe past her plastic planner, an ink pen and even a bobby pin, everything but the crinkled five dollar bill she remembers putting in her purse just last night.

Shaking her head and closing her eyes, she mumbles, "I guess I don't have it."

"Here, Ma, I got some money," David shouts.

Tara looks down at her son and the first thing she sees is a crisp ten dollar bill.

David counts the money, bill by bill, excited to show her what he has learned.

"Where'd you get that from?"

"I found it. I found it at school," he says, still counting away.

"You ain't find that much money at school. You stole it."

David freezes, his eyes staring hopelessly back at his mother.

"*Ma'am*," the cashier says.

Snatching the money from David and handing it to the cashier, Tara narrows her eyes at him.

"You betta be glad I ain't got a belt right here in this store. I'd whip you right now. Grab some bags, David."

David does as he is told, but fears the worst.

While riding on the bus, he is quiet, watching the cars pass by. *I hope she forgot about the money.* He fiddles with his fingers trying to control the fear rising up his chest. Looking up at his mother, he opens his mouth. "Ma, guess what?"

"What?" she snaps back.

"I got a eighty-two on my spelling test."

Tara turns to him. "Really?"

David starts to relax and almost smiles. "Yep!"

"That's good," she says with a slight smirk. She looks back at him and says, "Now back to this money."

David closes his eyes.

"You steal that money?" Tara asks again.

"No, Mom. I found it," David pleads.

"People just don't find money. You know that, right? You know I can't stand a thief."

David turns back to the window.

Tara yanks his head back, clawing his jaw bone. "Don't you turn from me when I'm talking to you."

"Yes, ma'am."

"So did you steal the money?"

David thinks about it for a second.

Smack.

The palm of her hand connects with the side of his face.

Tara looks up at the glass mirror above the bus driver. She is staring him down.

"Now you lucky we in public. Give me a damn answer," Tara whispers.

"A man gave it to me at the store," David quickly says, holding the reddening part of his face.

"A man ain't gonna just give you money. Since you still insist on lying to me. I'll just have to tell your father. I don't want to, but I be damned if my son goes to jail for stealing."

"No, Mom. No. I promise," David whines.

Tara looks into David's eyes. They are red and full of tears.

"I still don't believe you."

David slowly puts his head down.

As Sheri pulls up in her pearl white Cadillac, she sees Tara and David with their overstuffed bags as they take their final steps to their front door. She waves. "Hey, neighbor!"

Tara forms a semi-smile while sliding the key into the door knob. "Hi."

Sheri parks the car and nods her head. "Geesh, why do you have to be so angry at the world? Life is good," she mumbles.

She dips down into her gigantic trunk full of groceries and yells, "Daniel! Don't forget the eggs."

Once in the house, Sheri passes her chiming grandfather clock and the oil painting of her family and settles in the kitchen to unpack her groceries. She looks around the room, searching for the produce that needs immediate attention.

"That's my son," she says staring at the abandoned bags at the front door.

Sheri lifts the first bag off of the floor and onto the counter. It is orange juice. The most expensive, freshly-squeezed orange juice, no pulp and not from concentrate. She then pulls out her organic lettuce and immediately begins to tear each leaf from its stalk. Carefully pulling the red, ripe tomatoes out of the brown paper bag, she places them onto the counter and then pulls out her deli-wrapped Flounder.

"Daniel, get ready for baseball practice," Sheri yells. "Your cleats are already at the door!" She then begins to hum. She pours a capful of apple cider vinegar into the sink to wash off the lettuce and then grabs the lettuce spinner so she can keep her salad nice and crisp throughout the week. She pauses. "What's that noise?"

While holding a tomato under running water, she turns her head to the muffled scream. Her face scrunches up; she is confused. Her body stiffens as she is trying to be as quiet as possible to get a good listen.

Then she hears the sound again. It's sporadic, but much louder. Slowly, she turns the faucet off, and tiptoes to the kitchen window. She lifts it just enough to still be discreet, yet be able to hear clearly.

The hollering gets louder. It is a child's cry. David's, she assumes. Then, she hears a deeper voice. It's much clearer. "Shut the fuck up before I give you something else to cry about."

Sheri's thoughts scramble as she tries to decipher Tara's screams for Thomas to stop and David's cries. *What in God's name is going on in there?* Pulling the sheer curtains together and then hiding behind a corner of the window, she stands there with her ear as close to the opening as possible. She can now hear the pain clearly projecting through the opening of her window. The sound paralyzes her for a second. Her eyes are wide, her eyebrows raised, and her heart is beating rapidly as she holds her hands to her chest. *I have never.* She looks over to the phone with its spiral yellow cord dangling against the wall. *Maybe I should call...* She wrestles with the idea for a second, still sitting up halfway on the counter to hear. *Jacob's right. I should just stay out of their business,* she reasons.

After standing there for a while, the sounds of violence becomes too much for her to bear. She carefully closes the window and tries to ignore it. She tries humming, singing, and then even turns on some classical music. But it doesn't stop. Neither does the stiffening of her body. Even when she thinks it's over, she can still hear the noises ringing in her head; the screaming, the cries for help. They are loud and clear. She wrestles with the thought of possibly helping, while sliding the knife into the tomato, splitting it open, and tossing it into her crisp, chopped salad.

David lies down in his bed with his blanket fully covering his aching body. He's imagining himself as a little bigger and a bit heavier boy who lunges at his father with a kitchen knife. His daydream ends with warm tears rolling down his face, into his ears, and finally resting onto his pillow.

Suddenly the door opens. It scares him stiff. With one quick wipe, he erases his tears. He closes his eyes as if he is expecting something to happen. He relaxes his body to look asleep, except for his jittery eyes that he wishes so badly he can get under control.

There are footsteps coming in, walking closer and closer to him. Under the thick blanket and even with his eyes closed, he can see the light shine. A hand pulls back the covers, exposing cold air and the bright hallway light to his face.

He opens his eyes just enough for his pupils to see without fully opening them. It's his mother. David yawns, opening up his eyes just a little bit, just enough to clear his vision for a second. He can now see his mother's face. It's swollen. One eye is closed shut with juices oozing out. Her lips are double their normal size and smeared dried blood is on her ear. Tara bends down and kisses him. She barely presses down against him, but gets so close that he can feel the heat from her breath. His heart beats faster as he is trying to control the sudden quickness of his lungs. He watches her as she stares at him, wiping her tears and trying her hardest not to break out into an uncontrollable cry. She rubs his hair like he is a crying baby, never uttering a word.

David closes his eyes, clenches his jaw, and then takes deep breaths. After giving David one last kiss, Tara walks out of the room, closing the door as quietly as possible. Once the door is shut, he looks over at it and mumbles, "He's not going to change, Momma. He's not going to change."

David lies there for a second and then, like boiling water on the stove getting hotter and hotter, he sits up straight and allows the built up steam to release. He takes his pillow and throws it against the wall. He buries his head into his blanket and screams. Biting down on the ear of a teddy bear, he squeezes it and pulls it as hard as he can. He stares at the white naked wall in hopes of conjuring up a gun, a brick, or anything sharp. *I hate him. I hate him. I wish he would die.* He lies back down, mad at himself. Deep down he hates himself. He hates himself for not doing anything. He hates himself for not being stronger and he hates that he cannot protect his mother, especially after she tried to protect him.

"Just wait until I get older," he promises himself.

With a heart full of anger, hurt, and pain, and with nothing to do with it, he just swallows it whole.

After taking a deep breath and after his breathing eases, he thinks about KG. He thinks about how everyone respects him, how he is fearless, the wad of money, the beautiful girl, and the power.

Like a mental slideshow, David sees images of the humungous homes his friends own, their big yards, their fathers with great jobs. He hears Daniel and his father jumping on the trampoline, laughing and having fun, throwing the ball into the basketball hoop.

"I have to get money. That's the only way my mother can move far away from my dad. It's the only way," David says, shaking his head.

David closes his eyes tight; it helps him focus his thoughts.

"Daniel's party!" he thinks. He opens up his eyes. They are sore and dry, but bursting with hope.

They got money.

David sits up in his bed, fully awake now.

I can snatch something up and sell it. Just like my cousin taught me. They'll never know. He wipes the last tear from his cheek.

I just can't get caught.

CHAPTER SEVEN

Down to the last minute, Sheri is throwing up blue and white streamers, draping satin blue tablecloths around her end tables, and harassing the baker about Daniel's expensive birthday cake. From the street signs to the front door, there are blue and white floating balloons and on the front porch there is a banner that reads, "Happy Birthday, Daniel. We love you."

Ding dong.

Sheri rushes to the door. She pauses in the mirror, puts on a smile and then tugs at her blue, tight-fitted dress. "Is everything perfect, Jacob?" she asks.

Jacob glances at his wife. The look is so fast, that all he really catches are the sparkles shining off the dress as she spins around like a princess going to a ball. "Sure, everything is fine," he says nonchalantly.

Sheri opens the door and extends her smile. "Hi, Debbie."

Debbie, who lives up the hill in the richest parts of Garrison Heights, stands there with a huge smile of her own. She's holding a square wrapped present that's overflowing with pearl colored ribbon and her middle child Toni is standing beside her.

"Welcome. You are the first to arrive," Sheri says. She waves at them, and walks them toward the kitchen. "We have plenty of food, drinks and..." Sheri then points downstairs. "The basement is where the children are going to be entertained. We hired a magician, Peter the Clown, air brush tattooist, balloon twisters and there's so much food down there, it could last for days." Sheri stops to wink at Debbie. "And the adults will be entertained up here."

Ding dong.

Outside her door is a group of people waiting in line like they are waiting to get into a club. The adults are anxious to start drinking, while the children are ready for some cake and ice cream. Amongst the newest arrivals are their neighbors Thomas, Tara, and David. At first they were not coming. However, once the decorations started coming up and the music began to blast, Thomas decided that maybe it wouldn't be such a bad idea to just check it out.

David stands in front of the tables that are full of gifts in awe, while Tara joins the women in the kitchen and Thomas sits next to Jacob to watch a boxing match.

"Happy birthday, Daniel!"

David whips his head to the front door. He knows that voice. It is Sam. She is wearing brand new leather boots with a zipper dangling on the side, red stockings and a Tommy Hilfiger jean dress. He can barely recognize her. Her smile is brighter than usual and her hair is blown straight instead of the natural curly waves. All eyes are pointing at her and her stepmother, Courtney, who has an expensive bag draped from her arm.

David studies Daniel and Sam. Sam's smile is bright as she hands Daniel a gift half her size. David looks down at his small present that is wrapped in the Sunday newspaper. He then looks up at the presents that resemble the shiny gifts displayed at the mall during the holidays and nods his head.

"Thank you," Daniel says, looking back at David with a boastful smirk.

"You're welcome," Sam says.

All of a sudden David feels a thump on the back of his head. "Boy, didn't I teach you not to stare at people," his father says.

Courtney pushes Sam gently through the doorway and says hello to everyone in the room, but she only receives a couple of dry "hi's" from the ladies and fully focused eyes from the men. She is turning heads. With her beautiful free flowing pants suit, her chocolate brown lip gloss, and her plump breasts, the men can't help but look.

Courtney struts pass them. From the corner of her eye, she sees them turn their head and drool over her shapely figure. All the men except one - Jacob. She tries waving to him, but his eyes never stray away from the television screen. She tries slowing her walk down while right in front of him, but he turns the other way.

Already half drunk, Jacob avoids connecting eyes with Courtney or her sensuous sway at all costs. In fact, he is so buzzed that he probably won't remember telling Thomas that he was going to put in a good word for him for a dispatcher position at the police department.

In the kitchen, Courtney is met with cutting eyes and jealous stares. However, Sheri wastes no time in welcoming her.

"Hello, Courtney. You look *fabulous*. Where did you snatch up such a cute purse?" Sheri rubs the leather purse, lifting it up to examine its authenticity. "What a beautiful bag." The other ladies just shake their heads. Just a half hour ago, Sheri was dishing gossip and Courtney was the first name that popped out of her mouth.

She extends her French manicured fingers out to the food. "You all can start eating," she says, walking towards the blender. "I'll start the margaritas and then—"

Out of the blue, Sheri stops talking. She extends her neck out toward the window. "I heard something," she whispers.

"Don't take my car! Please don't. Don't take my car!" There are voices coming from outside. Sheri's face immediately scrunches with curiosity. "Is that Ramona? It sounds like Ramona," she says. She rushes out of the kitchen, stumbling over her friend's foot to get outside. The other guests quickly follow.

Outside on the porch the ladies watch in awe. The dark sky is lit up with bright flashing lights. They are reflecting off of every house and car on the street.

"Mommy, why are they taking our car?" two blond kids scream from their bedroom window. Their voices travel along the quiet streets. It reaches the ears of all of the neighbors who are standing around whispering amongst each other and staring back at the scene.

Downstairs, through a basement window, Daniel, David, and Sam also watch.

"What are they doing?" David asks Daniel.

While Daniel's eyes are still glued to the action, he says, "They are taking their car. My mom said they can't pay for it anymore."

Across the street, in the yard, Ramona sits on the bottom step of her porch. She watches her husband move fast with a black trash bag in his hand. He is quickly throwing whatever he can in the bag before they tow the car away.

Sheri eyes the frantic woman and her husband Roger. She shakes her head, holding the palm of her hand to her mouth. "That is just so sad. Wow," she mumbles. She narrows her eyes at the guys with black bandanas wrapped around their bald heads.

One is standing beside Roger and the other behind the car with his chest poking out. While looking at the children who have now run down to the car and who are chanting, "Don't take our car!" Sheri nods her head again.

The kids are in their pajamas, which are covered with yellow smiley faces over a dark blue pattern. They are screaming with tears streaming down their little cheeks. Ramona swoops up her children. They fight, they kick the air, and they continue to scream, "Daddy. Don't let them take our car."

"I can't take this anymore," Sheri says, walking back into the house. At the sound of the diesel truck running and the car being lifted onto the trailer, the other women shake their head and walk back into the house, too.

All of the women gather around the kitchen's island. Sheri is the first to open her mouth. She looks around at the sad-faced women and excitement shoots through her. She starts by shaking her head. "It's sad how they are losing their house, too."

The silent room is broken with sighs, mumbles and "no's."

"Yes. Roger just lost his job," Sheri continues. "He was an electrician for the city." She shakes her head and gently taps the salt shaker against the table. "What's really sad is that Ramona was a teacher at Garrison Heights Elementary."

Teresa, a woman from the far corner of the kitchen makes her way to the center. "I knew I recognized her," she said, excited to finally get a word in. "She used to tutor the slow kids."

Sheri enjoys the attention. She can tell by the wide eyes that she is entertaining them. "Yes, they told her she should check out East Mount Elementary school. They're always short of teachers." Sheri turns around and grabs a handful of ice cubes from the freezer. "She came over here crying. It hurt me to see her like that. Anyway. She went there for a job interview." Sheri twists her face. "She said the school was full of loud, obnoxious kids, and the teachers...they looked stressed and miserable. She goes to her interview and gets the job. But," she says with great enthusiasm, "once they told her that her pay would be half of what she earned at Garrison Heights, because they are low on funding, she turned it down." She pauses and then a thought pops up. "Oh. Did you know that the whole school is on free lunch?" She shakes her head. "Shucks, I wouldn't want to work there either."

Tara cuts her eyes at Sheri. "Hold up. Don't be talking about East Mount. My son went to East Mount."

Sheri looks back at her dumbfounded. The tone of her voice heightens, "Oh. I didn't mean to..." Sheri looks at the other women for support. "I apologize."

Tara's twisted lips relax. She sits back down on the leather stool, folds her arms and stares at Sheri.

On the step, David listens carefully. He tilts his head from the sudden memory in his head. He mumbles, "That was Mrs. Bradley. She was a nice teacher." He shuffles his butt on the hard wooden step. "She always told me that if I did good in school, it would pay off."

The music is loud, everyone is either borderline tipsy or drunk, and the kids are having a ball. Thomas and Jacob are in the living room talking about the fight, while the women are in the kitchen sharing recipes and conversing about everybody on the street.

Everyone is so busy filling their bellies with food, daiquiris, and vodka that checking on the kids is the last thing on anyone's mind. Most of the kids are being entertained by the paid help. They are yelling and screaming, running around and breaking things. No one notices the birthday boy and his two best friends slip away out of plain sight.

Daniel climbs up the steps to the first floor and scans the scene. All he can see and hear are drunk women stumbling to the bathroom and the loud mouths of laughter, people talking over each other and the boom box's bass shaking the floor. "Coast is clear," he whispers down to his friends. He looks down at David and Sam, who are waiting by the steps for the signal. He waves for them to come up. The three tiptoe from the doorway of the basement to the bathroom. From the bathroom, they walk along the wall and finally make it to Daniel's room.

Once David walks into Daniel's room, he is struck with awe. He can't believe all of the toys and gadgets Daniel has sitting around still in their original packaging.

"Man, if that was mine, I would open it up as soon as I got it," David mumbles.

From the miniature pool table to the row of remote control cars, David's eyes are busy trying to keep up. There is just so much going on. All four walls are painted dark blue. There is a mural of

Dale Earnhardt's race car on one wall and life-size baseball decals on the others. It is nothing like David's four white walls that have nothing but dirty smeared fingerprints on them. David looks at Daniel's king-size bed that sits up high, a desk with a stack of books on top of it, and one of those chests that looks as if it holds a wealth of secret treasures. It is all amazing to him. It even smells good to David; it's a mix of fresh leather and new packaging.

Sam is the first to plop down onto Daniel's pillow top mattress. Then David follows. They both watch Daniel as he goes inside his closet to dig something out. "I'm going to show you something, but you can't tell anyone," Daniel says.

After standing on a stack of wobbly Encyclopedia books and almost falling, Daniel finally pulls out a cardboard box with a huge white Nike Check printed on the lid. He kneels down on the floor. With his back turned to his door, he looks at his curious friends. Slowly and with much care, he opens the box. The feeling of his adrenaline pumping and his heart racing is overwhelming. It's fear, mixed with excitement. Just looking at their anticipating stares makes him giddy inside. He uncovers the lid. Then looks at them. No reaction. He is puzzled by their blank expression, their dumbfounded, confused looks. They are waiting for the huge surprise.

"What is it?" David says, bending down from the bed and trying to get a closer look.

Daniel lifts a baggie of light colored rocks with one hand and then grabs the foggy glass tube and puts it in the palm of his other.

"It's crack. Duh," Daniel says, irritated that the kids are not as excited as he is.

The two on the bed are mesmerized. They have only heard their parents talking about it. They are only familiar with the term 'crackhead,' but to be sitting right there in front of it, they are stuck. They are waiting for something to happen.

CHAPTER EIGHT

"I think they're in Daniel's room, yeah, that's it," Jacob yells to Thomas, pointing to the Jordan picture hanging on the door. Thomas leans into the door. He turns the knob slowly.

Daniel hears the door as it cracks open and jumps from the squeaking sound. While fumbling with the pipe, he drops it. He then picks it up as fast as he can and throws it under the bed, kicking the bed skirt to make sure it's hidden.

"What y'all doin' in here?" Thomas says, walking into the dark room.

"Nothing!" they say in unison.

Daniel, David, and Sam are all frozen, scared to budge.

Thomas narrows his eyes at them.

"Okay, David." Thomas looks at his son. "What are y'all doing in here?"

With fear in his heart and bullets of sweat about to break through his skin, David takes a hard swallow. He's afraid to breathe, only taking shallow breaths. His body is going numb and his mind is not working properly.

Still sitting in the living room, Jacob notices that Daniel's door is closed and Thomas has disappeared. He sets his beer down, clacking it onto the glass table, and gets up to check things out.

"Well, did you find–," he says opening the door. The first thing he sees is three scared children on the bed with a macho-looking man staring down at them.

"What's the problem?" Jacob asks.

"The problem is that these three here are hiding something."

All eyes land on Daniel.

"Daniel, what's going on in here?" Jacob asks.

"Nothing, Dad."

"All right, forget the bull," Thomas interrupts. "I think I know where it's at."

Thomas steps over Daniel's head, kneels down on one knee, lifts the bed skirt up, and pulls the cardboard box from under it. As soon as the light hits it, Thomas recognizes the hard rock.

"What the–" He twists the bag around and presses down on it to inspect the texture. "Crack?"

Thomas looks up at Jacob.

Jacob's face is blank. "Where did that come from?" Jacob asks. "It can't be ours."

"What? What you tryna say?" Thomas stands up tall, hovering over Jacob. He stares Jacob down.

Jacob stares back. He opens his mouth, "I–"

Before Jacob can spit out his next word, Thomas lunges at him like a tiger on its prey and starts punching him in his face.

Blood wastes no time in gushing out of his nose and trickling everywhere as Jacob tries to block his punches. Jacob takes a step back and wipes the blood from his cut. He gathers himself as

Thomas eggs him on with his hands. "Come on. Come on, man. You want more?"

After hearing all of the commotion and ruckus, the whole house gathers around the doorway to witness the altercation. No one is brave enough to intervene. Jacob catches Thomas with a two piece, and then everyone watches as Thomas wrestles him down to the floor. Jacob and Thomas are punching and elbowing each other like two enemies on the street.

Sheri stands there, shocked. Standing there like a zombie trying to figure out what is going on, she holds her hands up to her mouth.

"I'll call the police," one of the guests blurts out.

Those words are magical to the men. Like a spell that has been cast on the two enemies, they immediately stop swinging at each other.

"Naw, we good. We good!" Thomas says, stepping back from Jacob, but still keeping an eye on him.

"Yeah. We can handle it," Jacob adds.

The thought of violating his parole snaps Thomas back into reality, while getting his co-workers involved in the case of the mysterious stone squashes Jacob's motivation to fight.

"Get out! Everybody get out!" Jacob yells.

Daniel is the first to dart out of the room. He sprints down to the basement and doesn't turn back.

Thomas snatches David up with one arm and heads out of the door. Sheri, who is still dumbfounded, backs away from the room, while the rest of the guests quickly exit the house. Some take a pit stop just long enough to grab a couple of plates and others are slick enough to grab a couple of bottles before leaving. When the house is clear, Jacob yanks Sheri into Daniel's bedroom.

Once in the room, Jacob picks up the box from the floor and shoves it into Sheri's hands. "This was in Daniel's room!" Jacob throws her to the floor and slams the door.

"I thought you said you had it under control," he whispers. He shakes his head. "How did you go from coke to smoking crack, Sheri?"

Jacob looks at his wife's bloodshot eyes. She is helpless on the floor. She squints and jumps with his every movement.

Jacob kneels down to her. He moves in closer to her and whispers, "What are you doing? Sheri, what are you doing?"

Sheri sits up just enough to whisper into his ear. "What are *you* doing?"

Jacob looks at Sheri with confusion plastered on his face. He squints his eyes to get an understanding.

"I know you bought Courtney that purse and the clothes her daughter is wearing," she says. She narrows her eyes at him. "And I know why."

With fresh cuts and bruises covering his face and his left eye swelling up by the minute, Jacob rings the doorbell to Thomas's house. He waits a second, kicking loose gravel under his feet, and then rings the doorbell again. The throbbing pain in his face worsens. He gently tries to measure the swelling by pressing against his face. It's too painful. He steps up to the door once more and rings the bell. This time he gets an answer.

Jacob looks up at Thomas through the screen. He looks him straight in the eye. "Look, I apologize for what happened, man. I should have never accused you or your family. It's just..." He shakes his head in disbelief that he is even having this conversation. "Well, my old lady, she has a problem, and I was shocked to see - you know - the problem sitting in the hands of my son." Jacob closes his eyes in hopes of somehow it helping to erase the image. In doing so, a tear slips out. He plays it off by turning away and rubbing his nose. "I don't mean any disrespect. I just wanted to tell you face to face, man to man."

Thomas's hardened face softens. Surprised by the apology, he extends his hand out. "You cool, bruh. You cool."

Jacob attempts to crack a slight smile. His facial muscles refuse to budge. He nods his head and walks back to his house wondering how he is going to put back the pieces to his family.

Thomas closes the door and calls for David.

David is shaken, scared, and ready to take a beating. His footsteps stop a couple of feet away from his father.

"I said come here," Thomas repeats.

David lifts his head and slowly puts one foot in front of the other, looking like a lost puppy dog.

Thomas grabs his son and throws his arms around him.

"I love you, son."

The words are so foreign to David, they scare him.

Tara stands there shocked, too.

Neither David nor Tara knew that while they were hiding from Thomas's anger after the party, he was sitting in the bathroom with tears rolling down his face.

He was thinking of his past. The first image he saw was the image of his mother kneeling down on the bed moving her head up and down between a man's legs. He can see himself - the five-year-old innocent boy watching it. He can still remember the smell of crack burning, the look the man gave him as he was being pleased by Thomas's mother. He looked at his mom. The once beautiful, soft-spoken woman who had tucked him into bed earlier. She didn't look at him. She didn't even know he was there. At that age, he often wondered if she even knew she had a son.

The next image was of his father. The last memory he had of him. He was cold, lifeless, and lying in a casket full of pictures of the handsome man he used to be. Thomas's young eyes couldn't even recognize the man he used to call dad. His face was disfigured, darker than usual. Then, a couple of nights after the funeral, his little ears heard the reason why he was dead. As his mother shot up in the bathroom, Thomas listened from the bottom of the door to her argument with his dead father. She was crying. Her voice was wavering. "You should have never robbed them." She answered herself back. "I don't care," she shouted. "You should have never took their–"

Thomas looks David square in his eyes. He doesn't blink, flinch, or hesitate. "I don't ever want to see you even looking at drugs. That shit's bad. Real bad." He lets David go. Feeling uneasy about his vulnerability, he yells, "Now go to bed."

That night, after watching Thomas deal with her son, after seeing the side of him that she saw when she first met him, she closes her eyes, and listens to him sleep. Placing her hands on his waist gently, she smiles. Then she prays. "Lord, I just want to thank you. If anyone could change him, I knew that it had to be you. Thank you, Jesus."

On a hunch, Tara gets out of bed. She had remembered seeing the flashing light on the phone signaling a missed call and a voicemail message. Quietly she picks up the phone and listens to the message.

"My name is Cathy. I am an honor student at St. Agnes High School - a senior next year. I tutor children over the summer with a program I am a part of called 'It Takes a Village.' I was referred by someone who is close to my heart, and I would love to mentor David."

The next morning, Tara calls Cathy. "Hello, this is Tara, David's mother. I was returning your phone call. Is my son doing that bad in school to where he needs a tutor over the summer?"

Cathy's voice projects so softly through the phone. "No, ma'am. It's not even like that. It's more of a mentoring program, to help guide him to college and for him to have a role model. I had a mentor, my mother, brother, we are a family that believes strongly in empowering young people."

Tara holds the phone between her ear and shoulder. She pauses. She looks up to the ceiling and comes to a conclusion. "Look, I don't have a car," Tara says.

"No problem, ma'am. I have a car, and I will pick him up and drop him off. I can do it on Mondays, Wednesdays and Saturday mornings."

Impressed, Tara nods her head. "Mmm. Okay. All right. But I have to meet you first."

"No problem," Cathy says.

CHAPTER NINE

It's finally the first week of summer. Daniel is throwing his clothes and game system in his suitcase and leaving with his grandfather to Florida. Sam is at the library talking to a librarian about a summer mentoring program, and David is watching Daniel from his bedroom window, thinking about how his summer is going to be full of boring chores and days of tiptoeing around the house to avoid a whipping.

"Mommy, can I go to camp?" he says, using his worn teddy bear as the mother.

"No. We don't have money for that," he says, moving the bear's head.

"*Boy,* I barely got money to feed you," he says, mimicking his mother's voice.

He looks at the teddy bear, loosens the grip on its neck, and allows it to drop onto the floor. David moves his head while he imitates his mother. "I have bills. Boy, did you know that the lights are about to get cut off? We might lose the house because we behind on our rent - and you sitting here asking me for a damn dollar for some candy." He moves his head with more emphasis, slowing down on certain words. "How many times do I have to tell you? We don't have any money. I don't have money for no science field trip, no money for a science fair, I just ain't got it. You will be okay. I didn't have money growing up either. We found things to do."

After his improv is done, he looks down at a blue piece of paper his teacher passed out in class on the last day of school. In

73

big white letters it reads, "Science camp (Take a dive into the world of marine biology and oceanography or spend a day uncovering secrets of ancient civilizations) only $75 per week."

David smacks his lips. He grabs a pen and starts drawing circles. But then once he starts replaying all of the reasons why his mother would say no, he starts digging the pen into the paper, stabbing it and then pulling away at the hole that had formed. He rips it into two. He picks up the torn pieces, balls them up, and then throws it at the window.

I wish we had money like Daniel. Then maybe I could go to Florida, or maybe even Disney World.

"David!" Tara says, peeking through his bedroom door.

Her voice scares him. He sits up straight and cracks a smile.

"David, get dressed. There is a girl coming over to meet you. She will be your tutor for the summer." Tara leaves the room.

"Ah, man," David complains.

Through the kitchen window, David watches a brand new silver Camry pull up into his driveway. The rims shine like they have just been detailed and the new paint job sparkles under the sun. The music is mellow, but dies as the girl opens her car door.

"Yes, ma'am. I promise I will take good care of him. He is in good hands," Cathy says.

David studies her as she talks, looking at her long, flowered dress that flows down to an inch above her red high heels.

"To be honest, Cathy," Tara says, "I am happy that my son is going to be around someone like you. Someone who is focused, motivated, and who is active in the community." She then nods her head with regret. "I sure wish I was thinking about my future when I was that young. Shoot. I wish someone like you would have come along and mentored me. The streets was my teacher. A very dedicated and loyal teacher." Cathy starts to look uncomfortable, shuffling her butt in the chair. "Well," Tara says scratching her scalp with her index finger. "I guess that's it."

Cathy glances at David and smiles. "Ma'am. It was nice meeting you. I will see you both on Saturday at one o'clock."

David continues to stare at her. He can't seem to turn away. He watches her as she stands up and walks toward the door. He smiles. He hasn't been so happy or smiled so much since… he met KG.

While outside, David waves goodbye to Daniel, who smiles back at him in the backseat as heads to Florida. "Maybe this is going to be a different summer, a fun summer."

Tara pats David on the head. "Maybe it is."

Daniel has finally arrived in Cherry Hills, Florida; it's a great day to take a dip in the community pool or to go relax under the shade of a tree at the park. However, none of these activities interest him. Surrounded by nothing but retired elderly people and snooty kids, Daniel is anxious to leave the gated community and see what Florida really has to offer.

"Hey, Gramps, can I go to Geauga Lake?" Daniel asks, walking into the tall, elegant living room. Daniel has just seen a commercial advertising the park's latest roller coasters and safari attractions. He looks over at his gramps. By the way he is fighting the air with his fist and scrunching up his face, it's apparent that something has him all worked up.

"Ignorance, ignorance I tell you," his gramps yells to the television. His veins are bulging from his neck and his face is growing red.

Daniel inches his way toward him, trying to see what has gotten him in a rage and then kneels down on the floor beside his chair.

The news is on. A tall reporter dressed in a blue business suit holds the microphone up to the lips of a black woman with a colorful hair scarf wrapped around rows of plump pink rollers. "I don't know what the hell happened," the woman says. "All I know is that I left and came back and they asses were laid out on the floor. The floor was full of blood," the woman tells the reporter as she adjusts her bra. She smacks her lips and rolls her eyes.

Gramps sees her face and becomes livid. "Those damn ignorant niggers."

Daniel's jaw drops. His eyes are stuck on the TV screen. He is so in shock that he's afraid to turn toward his gramps. Looking at the TV screen, he sees two black women. He is confused by the word. Daniel shuffles the word in his mind. *Nigger. Is that the same as nigga?* He thinks about the first time he used the word.

It was a day he was riding in the car with his father. Daniel had gotten all pumped up and excited about knowing all of the words to a song.

"What did you say?" his father asked. Daniel looked confused. "Don't say that word," Jacob said.

"What word?" Daniel asked.

Daniel remembers how his father pushed on the brakes, pulled over into the Dave's Supermarket parking lot, and stared him down like a criminal.

"Nigger. Don't say nigger or nigga. I don't want to ever hear you use that word."

"Why?" Daniel asked.

At a loss for words himself, Jacob just said, "You know your great - great. Shucks, I don't know how far back it was. I try not to think about it. He owned slaves." Jacob combed his fingers through his hair. He sighed. "The n-word is like calling someone a really bad name. It's a word that has a horrible history. You should never use a word like that, unless you know its history. Just like you should never judge a person without first knowing their history. Everyone has a history. Everyone has a reason why they do things. Even Gramps. He has a history and even though I don't agree with everything he does, I know his history enough to understand why he is the person he is."

Daniel looked at his father's reddened face. "So if it's so bad, why do people say it in songs?"

Jacob chuckled. "Now that's a question I can't answer. Just promise me you won't use it."

Sitting there looking at Gramps, Daniel relaxes. There must be a reason why he acts the way he does. He shrugs his shoulders, forgets about the word, and then focuses on Geauga Lakes.

"Gramps!" Daniel shouts. But again, he doesn't get his attention.

"Everywhere I turn, I see a cursing ignorant nigger."

Daniel covers his ears as if to stop a bug from entering them. His Gramps stops in the middle of his rant and smiles.

"Those were the good old days," he says, turning to Daniel.

Daniel's face is blank. Unsure how to respond, he just stares at his gramps.

"Oh, give them their food, throw them into a ghetto, then we'll never have to deal with them again. Hell, that was unsuccessful," he says, becoming more irritated. "We still have to deal with them. They still ask for more. What more do you want from us? To pay for your housing, healthcare, for your kids to go to college for free! Oh, that's what we do already and they still find something to complain about."

At first when Daniel sat down, he was shocked and in awe. But after a half an hour of the rants, his body has now relaxed and the once piercing, hateful words become digestible.

"You ok, Gramps?" Daniel says patting him on his shoulder.

"Yes." His grandfather takes a sip of his iced tea and then forms a smile.

Once he sees his grandpa's blood pressure descend, Daniel decides to ask the question again.

"Eh, Gramps. I wanted to know if I can go to Geauga Lakes."

"Geauga Lakes?" his grandpa repeats. "Uh. Well, uh, I thought you didn't like that park. You said that it was for babies."

"I changed my mind. I want to give it another try," Daniel says.

Gramps looks at his grandson. It reminds him of Jacob when he was little; he'd beg on one knee to go to the carnival. "All right. I guess so."

Once Daniel enters the park with his gramps, he sees the usual: kids walking ahead of their parents, holding their animal souvenirs, and overpriced hotdogs being stuffed down their throats. It is just what he remembers, *borrring*.

"Hey, Gramps, I want to walk around," Daniel says, blocking the sunlight with the palm of his hand.

"Okay, we can do that."

Daniel looks at his aged grandfather, his cane and slow strides and says, "No, I mean by myself."

"I don't know about that, Danny, I think we should stay together."

Daniel pokes his bottom lip out.

"All right, all right. I guess you are getting older. I'll let you go off on your own," Gramps says.

Gramps digs deep into his pocket and pulls out a worn leather wallet and then lifts out a wrinkled one hundred dollar bill.

"Will this do?"

Daniel smiles. "Yep, thanks." He snatches the green paper out of his hand and starts to walk away.

"Now hold on, Daniel. I need you to meet me back here at seven, all right? I have to be home to take my meds. Be safe and if you need me, I will be right here," he says, pointing to a black metal bench sitting in front of the park's play area.

"Okay," Daniel replies with the purest tone he can come up with.

Daniel walks toward the men's bathroom. Then he turns back to give his gramps a hug.

"Thanks, Gramps," he says, squeezing him gently. He squeezes a laugh out of his gramps and then walks away. Daniel smiles. *Works every time.*

Daniel runs to the men's bathroom and takes a sip of water from the water fountain. From the corner of his eyes he can see his gramps's butt in the air slowly descending to the bench. Once he sees that gramps's attention is focused on the clear blue sky, the birds flying, and a pretty woman that has just sat next to him licking the running ice cream from her cone, Daniel turns around and walks right out of the park.

He stretches his hands toward the sky. "I'm free!"

The city is busy with cars and curious tourists filling the streets. *Mmm. I wonder what's down there.*

For as far as Daniel can see, he is walking down a nice beautiful street. The wall separating the park from the street is a beautiful white stone and there are colorful flower beds everywhere. However, the farther away he gets from the park, the more his body tries to warn him that he is walking into unfamiliar territory. Distracted by the flashing "The Seafood Joint" sign that he is focused on, he doesn't notice his heart beating faster. He doesn't notice that fewer and fewer tourists are around, and he misses the fact that the buildings are becoming more and more vandalized.

Daniel walks and walks until the once small sign is now larger than life. He crosses the street, walks a ways, and then turns down an alley. He follows the sign, never paying any attention to the gradual deterioration of his surroundings.

Daniel arrives at his destination, The Seafood Joint. It is much different than what he assumed it would be. There are men standing everywhere. As he walks, he has to hop around empty

McDonald's cups, beer bottles, and broken glass. Then when he looks up from the trash on the ground, his eyes stop at the thick bars that are stretched out on every window.

Now realizing his situation, Daniel rubs his sweaty palms against his pants leg. He wipes the beading sweat from his brow, takes a deep breath, and looks over at the distance he must walk to get to the front door of the restaurant. It has many obstacles. More than he would like. With the men standing around already staring at him and with the cars with loud banging sounds coming in and out of the parking lot, he is afraid to move. But the steady growl of his stomach encourages him to continue.

CHAPTER TEN

"What's up, dude?" a tall white man says to him. Daniel hesitates. "Hi."

At first, Daniel keeps his head down, but then his eyes wander up. His eyes start with looking at the man's tattooed arms, but once Daniel sees the man's hairy chest with blue ink that reads the words "Thug Life" on it, he quickly looks back down to the ground and rushes into the restaurant.

He feels a sense of relief. He enjoyed the adrenaline rush, the fear for his life. But he's relieved that it's over. However, once he sees the thick, dingy glass between him and the cashier, Daniel's fear resurfaces.

"What you want?" the man says through a couple of drilled holes in the glass.

"Um. I want a..." Daniel looks up at the red menu struggling to read its bright yellow letters.

"I want the...uh... I just want the fries."

"With or without sauce?" the cashier asks.

"Sauce. I guess," Daniel says.

Daniel pulls out his balled up bill, tugs at it to straighten it, and then looks for a place to pay the man. Everywhere he looks, there is nothing but thick glass.

The cashier laughs at the boy. "You can't be from 'round here." He taps on the counter. "Right here, dude. Right here."

Daniel puts his money under a deep opening in the counter and then turns to look outside. The white man outside is staring at him while the others are talking amongst themselves. Daniel's eyes move away from the white man and drifts over to a black man that's leaning against the brick wall. His heart pounds even harder. Daniel decides to just turn around and stare into the thick bullet proof glass until his fries are ready.

"Here's your change and here is your food," the cashier says, placing the brown bag into a swiveling glass door.

Daniel fumbles with the door. His hands are shaking. His teeth are chattering. Finally, he manages to grab the greasy bag. He tucks his change in his pocket as deep as it will go, almost creating a brand new hole, and walks back out into the parking lot.

He is moving so fast it's as if each leg is racing each other.

"Ay. You. Come here," a man calls out.

Daniel stops dead in his tracks, afraid to take another step. He looks at the street. *Do I run across the street?* His head turns at the speeding cars. *There is no way I am going to make it.* Afraid to turn around, he just stands there, frozen, like he's in a game of Red Light, Green Light.

"I know you hear me. Come here!" the man yells.

Daniel turns around slowly, his eyes moving toward the sound of the voice. It is the white man with the tattoos that's talking to him. Daniel takes in the thick humid air and moseys his way to the man. He doesn't say a word.

"Give me your money," he commands.

Daniel reaches down into his pocket and hands him the wrinkled bills.

The man chuckles. He quickly flips the bills, counting them one by one, and then stuffs them into his pocket. "Where you from?"

Daniel stutters. "I'm from, uh, Ohio."

"Ohio? That's far from here."

"Yes, I stay with my gramps."

The man bursts out laughing and looks at the others who are also cracking up.

"Gramps," he repeats.

"Where do 'gramps' stay?"

Daniel taps his temple with his finger. "I don't know. He lives somewhere in Cherry…Cherry…"

"Cherry Hills?" The man finishes the word, nodding his head slowly. "Okay, okay."

He licks his lips as if it is covered with sweet leftovers and ponders for a second. He rubs his hands together and then extends his hand out to shake Daniel's hand.

"I'm James," he says.

Daniel raises his eyebrow with confusion. He shakes James' hand anyway.

"Keep your money. But I want you to call me tonight at eleven o'clock. You are going to give me your gramps' address and tomorrow you're going to kick-it with me."

Daniel stutters. "You…you are going to pick me up?"

"Yep. We cool, right? You want to see the city. I'm going to show you."

He waves for the rest of the gang to come over and they all shake Daniel's hand.

"We good, right? We cool?" James asks.

"Yes," Daniel says with a smile.

Daniel is surprised and also a little leery. While walking back to the park, he thinks about the incident. *But they say they are cool, so they must mean it. Plus they gave me my money back.*

The walk back to the park is much different than when he was wandering off the first time. Every sound, crackle, and pop sends jitters through him. His heart is beating much faster. He doesn't know if it's because he is still shaken up or if it's from the excitement and anticipation of meeting up with James. *Eleven o'clock. I can do that. Eleven o'clock. What's the worst that can happen*

Back in Ohio, David climbs into Cathy's car. He watches as the scented plastic diamond dangles on the rear view mirror and then gazes out of the window at the passing cars.

"I told you I was going to pick you up at one o'clock sharp," Cathy says to David. "I always keep my word."

David looks at Cathy's dark sunglasses and smiles. He then relaxes in his seat as he studies the rest of the car; it's much different than riding the crowded city bus, full of sticky leather and the breath of a million souls. David feels the texture of the leather seats. He smoothes his hand along the shiny dashboard and his eyes widen at the bright lights coming from the radio. He even feels comfort in resting his elbow on the soft arm rest - something he could never do on a bus.

The view is different, too. On the bus, he is always higher up, looking down into the nice vehicles, wondering where the happy drivers and laughing kids in the back seat were going and wishing he were in their place. In the car, he was on the same level as everyone else, just the way he preferred it.

"This is nice," he says, nodding his head.

"So, David, what do you want to be when you grow up?" Cathy says.

The question throws him out of his daydream, out of the pleasure of just enjoying the smooth ride. It throws him back into reality, his real issues, and his real thoughts about his blurry future.

David looks down at the squeaky clean floor mat and says, "Um. I want to be a, um, doctor."

It is the first thing that pops up in his head. The image of a white doctor in a white coat and a silver round button like tool hanging from his neck. The image seems unrealistic. His heart beats as if he had just told a lie.

"Oh, a doctor, huh?" Cathy says as if she is proud of his aspirations. "That's cool. That's really, really cool. My parents are doctors. My mother is a neurologist and my father a pediatrician. Do you want to know what I am going to be?" Cathy says while spinning the steering wheel to make a wide turn.

David looks at her, more interested in her than ever. "What?"

David watches Cathy enter a cloud of dreams. Her voice heightens as she speaks, as she paints a clear picture for him.

"I want to become a lawyer. I want to be that powerful woman that everyone underestimates. I want to be a..." She pauses to smile. "A female version of Johnnie Cochran."

David can tell that she means what she says. He can tell by the words that flow effortlessly out of her mouth. He looks at her with admiration. Just being in her presence makes him feel like he can do anything. Seeing how this is the first time he has ever met anyone with such high expectations and goals, he starts to ponder. *Maybe I can be a lawyer.*

Finally they pull up into the driveway. It is the biggest house on the street, with a long circular driveway.

"That's where you live?" David asks with eyes as big as two golf balls flying in the air.

"Yep, that's where I live," Cathy says.

David can't believe it. It is the first time he has ever seen a house so big and owned by a person of his skin color. He has only seen black people live in the ghetto or only making it as far as the borderline of the suburbs. Even on TV, he rarely remembers ever seeing a black family in a big house like that. Only images of shiny rims and long chains seem to swirl around his mind when it comes to what black people are able to acquire.

"Are you going to get out of the car?" Cathy jokes, waiting for David.

"Oh, yeah."

He snaps off his seat belt and swings it to the side. He steps out of the car, allowing the warmth of the sun to fall on his face. The sun is shining bright and the grass is looking extra green with flowers blossoming everywhere.

Everything is perfect. Not one grass blade is taller than the other. From the water fountain rolling water to and from the top of the statue to the birds chirping, it all feels like a dream. Never in his life has he felt so at peace. They stroll through the large double doors and into the house.

"Come this way. We will study here."

They walk past the huge kitchen with a big island in the middle, a room that looks like someone went crazy with the color white and then into a room with a long polished wooden table in it. The table is set much like a home that he remembers seeing on *The Fresh Prince of Bel-air*, each plate and shiny utensil placed perfectly on its own burgundy cloth placemat.

David's eyes run rapid. He can't stop looking around. His eyes pause at the cool paintings and his hands are tempted to touch almost every interesting vase and sculpture in the house.

"Let's sit here and we can begin."

For an hour, Cathy takes David through the basics of phonics. She works with his syllables and encourages him to take his time to listen and to sound out each word. The whole time, David is having fun. He is full of laughs, cracking jokes and is anxious to sound out the words correctly. She takes her time with him. Butterflies flutter in his stomach.

"Ter...min..." David's head is buried in a book as he tries reading aloud; his head lifts up when he feels a hand land on his shoulder.

"What's up, li'l man?"

David drops the book down in his lap, not paying attention to the pain that the sharp edges have caused on his thigh.

"KG!"

David's face lights up. He can't scoot his chair back fast enough.

Dressed in a black suit and tie, no jewelry, no beautiful girl hanging around him, KG is almost unrecognizable to David. His lineup is razor sharp and his breath smells of cool peppermint candy. When he leans in to give David dap, he brings along with him a hint of cologne that screams masculinity.

"How'd it go?" Cathy looks up at him and asks.

"You already know," KG replies, walking away from the table with a huge smile.

Cathy smiles. Then yells to KG, "I bet you're going to be a lot more careful next time, huh?"

"You know it," KG says, disappearing into the hallway.

CHAPTER ELEVEN

S am sits Indian style on her pink flowered comforter with her mother's journal nestled in her hand. She thinks about how David is never home and how Daniel is off having fun in Florida and decides to read her journal for the hundredth time. At least it will hold her over until she gets to see Amina, her mentor.

Baby girl, Samantha, you are amazing. Today you just took your first step. I've watched you fall, I've watched you stumble and I've watched you stagger to your feet. But you always got right back up. You never gave up, baby. And now, my dear, you are walking.

Sam smiles at the words. Her body warms up with happiness. As she relaxes deeper into her pillow, the words from her mother's journal make her mother come alive, making it impossible to forget her soft voice and pleasant demeanor, then suddenly she hears a banging at her door.

"Open the damn door," a loud belligerent man commands, disrupting her peace of mind.

Bang. Bang. Bang.

The banging instantly throws Sam's whole body on guard. Her light brown eyes are bucked and her limbs rigid. The shallow door moves as its being beaten like a worn drum set.

She tries to ignore it. She tries to focus in on the words, flying through the sentences, allowing the words that are coming off of the pages to comfort her.

The Influenced

Today you have shown me that there is nothing in this world you can't do. You remind me of Aunt Betsy. She was strong, just like you. Hardheaded at times, but had a relentless spirit. She got it from her mother, who got it from her mother. You see, you come from a line of strong women. Each one of them stopped at nothing to get what they wanted out of life.

Bang. Bang. Bang.

"Give me the keys, give me the damn keys," the man yells at Courtney.

Sam listens to her stepmother scream behind her bedroom door, begging for him to stop, for him to leave her daughter alone. She stares at the golden padlock on the door.

Sam tries to remain calm, while sitting at the edge of her bed. She cannot stop her heart from pounding so hard. Her body is becoming tenser, her breaths deeper and her limbs are freezing up. However, it doesn't take long for her body to no longer allow her to ignore the danger. Her heart is beating too fast and she is on the verge of tears. She is even more fearful that at any moment somehow, someway the man is going to burst through the door.

"No, leave her alone," Courtney yells even louder.

Sam slams the journal down onto her bed and then runs into her closet. It's her safe haven within her safe haven. Tucked into the darkest place in the closet, behind a group of hanging clothes, she puts on her headphones. Closing her eyes and blasting the music as loud as possible, she drowns her thoughts with musical instruments so her mind can no longer wander with fear.

A couple of minutes pass and Sam's heartbeat has slowed. But then the darkness in the closet suddenly lights up. Even with her eyes closed, she can see a tall, dark silhouette inch toward her.

She opens her eyes. She looks up at the tall man. She screams. Her feet flutter trying to dig deeper into the closet, but there is nothing but a solid wall keeping her from crawling any further. The man jumps at her and yanks her from her hiding place. The headphones fall from her head and the sound of her CD player crashing down is just a faint worry in her mind. With much strength and quickness, he grabs her little arm, picks her up with one hand and even though she is kicking in midair, he slings her onto the bed. She screams again, but louder.

Frustrated, the man grabs his ears, trying to protect them from her high pitched shriek. "Shut up," he says, pinning her down.

"Stop! Stop!" her stepmother yells.

She tries pulling him off, but can't. There is no stopping this vulture of a man, especially a hundred pound woman that is as slim as a string bean. He is huge in every way. From his arms to his torso even down to his mighty strength. He is in total control of the situation. He yanks his pants down with one arm just enough to expose the top portion of his boxers and holds the screaming girl down with the other. She is squiggling. Tears are rolling from her eyes to the sheets and she is kicking wildly. But instead of deterring the monster from its prey, it makes him more excited and more determined. He pins her legs down with his thighs and then covers her mouth with his calloused fingers. As he pries her legs open, she can hear an angel, maybe a devil. It doesn't matter who it is; Sam is happy to hear it.

"Get the fuck off of my baby."

He stops, and then looks back at a long barrel aimed at his head. His arrogant smirk turns into a "Please don't shoot me." He pulls his pants up as fast as he can, throws his hands up, and waddles away from Sam.

"Get the fuck out of my house," Courtney demands.

Sam wipes away her tears and sucks in as much air as her lungs will allow. She sits up and looks at her stepmother with her scraggly hair and smeared makeup and her black stream of tears and is struck with awe. This is the strongest she has ever seen her since her father was killed.

She watches her stepmother walk out and then shut the door. Looking at the padlock, she wonders how in the world the man was able to get in.

She thinks back to what her stepmother instructed for her to do while a man installed the padlock. "If at any time, you feel unsafe, lock the door. Don't open it even for me. I don't care who it is or what they say. Never open it."

Confused and still flustered from what had just happened, a deeper fear crawls into Sam's mind, shakes her body, and makes her heart drop. Suddenly, the thick golden padlock means nothing to her. If anything, it is more like a prison now than ever before.

Sam writes on the back side of her mother's journal.

I am strong. I am strong. I am strong because my momma said so. I am strong because my grandmother was strong. My great grandmother was strong. I will always be strong.

After her mind clears, she opens the journal back up and continues to read it. She reads a lot slower, fighting the urge to stop reading to ball up and cry.

I don't know how old you will be when you finally read this journal, but I want you to do something for me. I want you to learn your history. If I am not there to teach it to you, you must do the learning yourself. You must walk your butt to the library and read about who you are. Only then will you grow up into the person you are supposed to be. But in the event something does happen, beg your father to take you. Even though he hates the library, there is nothing he wouldn't do for his little princess. Gotta go, your father is calling. Love you, Sweet Pea.

Sam shuts the book, closes her eyes, pulls the cover over her head, and then silently cries herself to sleep.

The next day, Sam catches the bus to a nearby university. She wears a smile despite her crazy night, but by the end of the day, she can't seem to keep it together.

"What's the problem?" her mentor from "It Takes a Village" asks after giving Sam some instructions.

With her head still down, Sam studies the different shades of brown carpet. "He said no," she mumbles.

"Oh, nuh uh. You will not!" Amina says, grabbing the arm of the chair and shoving it back under the table. "What you sitting down for?" Amina stands up and begins to wave her hands. "You, just like everyone in here, are entitled to go on the college tour. You have to speak up and command your respect. I don't care if it's an adult, a child, a dog, a pony, a rainbow."

A chuckle escapes Sam's lips.

"Sam, seriously," she says, laughing at herself. "It's important to use your voice."

Amina narrows her eyes and straightens her face. "Do you understand?"

After kneeling down by Sam's side, Amina points to a little girl sitting with her mother. "Do you see that little girl?"

Sam turns her attention to a girl her age who is talking to her mother.

"I can tell by her attitude that she gets what she wants. She's been taught that she deserves whatever this world has to offer."

Amina stops to poke Sam gently in the chest. "That's the confidence I need you to have. I understand you are used to being told no. You are used to being told to shut up when adults are talking to you and to accept no for a no."

Sam smiles, agreeing with her.

"I feel you. I was raised the same way. But you have to beat that mentality that you don't deserve what others have. You do. No more sad faces, no more pitiful looks to get what you want. You speak up and don't stop until you get a yes. All right?"

They both walk over to the man as he sips on his black coffee and bites into his cherry danish. Once they stop in front of the wooden table, Sam hides behind her mentor's full figure. But as fast as she falls back, Amina's arm swings her little body back in front.

"Sam, don't forget what we talked about," Amina says.

Sam raises her head up to the graying tour guide. With a projected voice, she straightens her hunched back, looks him straight in his eyes and says, "Why can't I go on the tour? If they can go, so can I."

Amina leans back on the wall with folded arms along with a smile on her face.

The man starts stuttering over his words while trying to come up with an excuse.

"Well. I…It may not be…" He looks over at the college students that are waiting for him. He shrugs his shoulders and says, "All right. You can come."

Sam looks at Amina and smiles.

"It will be a minute," the man says to Amina.

Amina points to Sam. "You can tell *her* that."

The man moves his eyes back down to Sam. "I'll let you know when we are ready to leave. If that's good with you?"

With a beaming smile and a cheerful spirit, Sam says, "Okay," making sure to speak up.

While the man walks away, Amina kneels down to Sam. She embraces her.

The feeling of a warm caring body stirs up Sam's emotions. She nestles her head onto Amina's shoulders.

To a rhythm, Amina rocks Sam back and forth in her arms. She is filled with inconceivable joy.

"I am proud of you," she whispers.

For a while there is silence, only the sound of the people passing by. As Amina holds her, Sam's body weakens and her breaths become deeper. She is sniffling. Amina pulls away from her to look her into her eyes. "What's wrong, Sam?"

Sam's face is covered with tears. There is snot running from her nose and she is breathing rather heavily.

"What's the matter?" Amina repeats.

Sam tries to spit the words out. But it only sounds like a mumble. "But my mom is dead. My father is…"

Amina pulls Sam back into her arms. She continues to rock her and talk to her.

"It's okay to cry. Cry until you can't cry anymore. Your mother is dead, yes. Your father is dead, yes. Your stepmother is on drugs. I know. Go ahead and cry. Cry until you're all cried out."

Sam bursts out into more tears. Amina squeezes her tighter and pats her on the back as Sam rests her head back into the dip of her shoulder.

Sam tries again to say what's been on her heart for years. "I just can't…"

Amina whispers the words slowly. "Nothing is going to change what happened. I can't change it, you can't change it, and neither can those tears."

She slowly wipes each tear off of Sam's face. "Life is hard, baby girl, and people will look at you and feel sorry for you. They will hand you things. But that's not how life works. It will only make you weaker. So soft that you will mold to whatever society says you can become. You will start feeling like you are not strong enough to just go out there and get it yourself."

Sam pulls away. "But…But." Her eyes are bloodshot red. "I don't have anyone."

Amina smiles at her. "You have me. I am going to help you grow strong in this crazy world. I am going to water you with encouragement like a delicate flower. I am going to nurture you until you become strong again." Amina puts up a finger. "But there is one thing I will need from you. I need you to find strength in your past and use it to deepen your roots. Stretch out and grow. Then touch someone else and help them grow. I don't want people to see you as a weak, pitiful woman broken up because of your past. I want them to see a strong, confident, and intelligent woman who demands the kind of respect she deserves. You will not fail." She pulls Sam away from her, looking deeply in her eyes. "I won't allow it."

CHAPTER TWELVE

David waits anxiously as Cathy pulls out a clear container full of laminated flashcards, a couple of books and games and slides it onto the table.

"David, what a difference a month has made," Cathy says. "You practice at home, don't you?"

"Yep, I count everything. I count my rice when I eat." He looks up at Cathy as she laughs. "I divide potato chips, and I multiply the marbles that you gave me. I did everything you said, CC."

David's legs swing in the chair as if he can't control them and he taps his hands against his thigh.

"I am so proud of you. You keep this up and KG is going to have a surprise for you."

"For me?" David asks.

"Yep, for you."

"Let's take a lunch break and then we can practice a little more reading."

Cathy then smacks herself on the head. "Oh, I forgot to tell you. *Shoot.* I'm going to have to take you home early today."

David's smile droops down to a frown. He smacks his lips and throws down the flashcards as Cathy walks to her room.

Still looking pitiful, David drags his feet to the over-sized stainless steel refrigerator. He glances at a picture that is stuck on the refrigerator with him and Cathy at a family reunion a couple weeks ago; he can't help but smile. "I love it here," he says to himself, rubbing the smooth laminated surface.

David scans the refrigerator for something to eat. He looks in the refrigerator so freely now. The first time he came to Cathy and KG's house, he can remember being surprised at how much food was stuffed in the refrigerator. But now, he just reaches in, grabs the bread, sliced deli ham, and then a Little Debbie snack for dessert.

"Ayyyy yooo," KG yells, walking through the front door. In his arms, he's carrying a small package. He glances into the white room to see if anyone is there and then throws the package on a hallway table.

He walks right past the kitchen, and when he sees a head pop up out of nowhere, he tenses up and jumps back, fists in the air. "Oh shit, David. I didn't even see you."

David runs over to him and gives him a big hug.

"What's up, my dude?" KG asks, giving him dap. "Where's CC?"

David jumps at the opportunity to answer the question.

"She's in her room."

"Tell her that I have a couple of runs to make and then I'll be back."

David hesitates for a second, looking down at the grooves in the hardwood floor. His heart beats fast and his fingers are rubbing the edges of his nail as he is trying to work up the nerve.

"Uhh. Can I go?" David asks with the biggest hope in the world. His face is displaying a semi smile, for he is preparing himself for a "no."

KG looks at David, looks down at his black Rolex watch and then studies the dimples in David's face. "I guess you can go. Hurry up though."

David hurries to the front door and grabs his shoes.

"I'll call CC when we get in the car," KG says.

This can't be real, David thinks to himself.

Close behind, David follows KG out of the house, admiring everything about him. From the way he walks, to the gold chains dangling from his neck; David smiles at him in admiration.

With a smile larger than life and with feet carrying him as fast as they can, David jumps into the black Bimmer, shuts the door, and watches his idol get in the car.

"You ready for a little ride?"

"Yep," David shouts.

The ignition kicks the engine up; the music starts blaring and the windows roll down just enough to catch a small flow of outside air. David loves it. There is no other place he'd rather be.

"Yeah, CC. I took little D with me. We going to ride to the East Side and then I'll be right back," KG says over the phone.

CC smacks her lips. "KG! I have to be somewhere in an hour. You are going to make me late!"

"He gon' roll with me today then," KG says.

David acts like he isn't listening, like he is busy looking out the window. But he can't help but to hear and to feel the effects of those words.

"Just call his mama and tell her you'll drop him off a little later. I'm sure she ain't gon' care."

CC smacks her lips, but then agrees to it. "You better make sure he comes back safe. All right?"

"I gotchu. Stop worrying about every damn thing."

KG hangs up the phone and then looks at David. David can see him from the corner of his eyes, but doesn't turn away from watching the cars roll past.

"You cool kickin' it with me?"

David turns his head and nods calmly. "Yep."

The first stop they make is to the Sunflower Valley Projects. It is a ways out from KG's house, about 30 minutes, but somehow David recognizes it. He doesn't quite remember why, but he remembers the brick sign with the large black letters, and the park with the playground in the middle.

KG pulls up into the large parking lot right in front of one of the gigantic buildings and opens up his door.

"I'll be back. I'm locking the door. Don't open up the door for nobody, ya hear?"

David nods.

KG steps out of the car. As he is walking to the sidewalk, a gang of men flock around him.

David watches as they exchange words and nod their heads. They are all huddled up and listening to KG like a football team plotting their next strategy.

David can tell that KG is in charge. Just from their body language alone, it is obvious that KG is the leader of the pack.

The next couple of stops are the same. KG gets out of the car, demonstrates the game plan, and then he is back into the car.

"You hungry?" KG asks.

David nods his head. He then grabs his rumbling stomach. Stop after stop, he wanted to say something, but the thought always disappeared once KG got back into the car.

"I'm going to take you to this soul food spot over on Shawny," KG says.

KG speeds up, swerves in and out of traffic, and then pulls out a Swisher. David is enjoying the ride. He feels the car as it accelerates to a hundred miles an hour. He gets scared when the cars they are passing seem to mesh with each other. He closes his eyes, but loves the sound of the rumbling engine, the vibration and lightness of the tires.

Once they arrive to the soul food restaurant, David is more than ready to get out of the car.

They both walk in, find a seat and pick up the menu full of chicken, collard greens, homemade macaroni and cheese, and even black eyed peas.

"Get whatever you want," KG says.

David is not used to this kind of treatment. He scans the menu and decides he wants the pork chops. The picture of the smothered pork chops, cheesy macaroni and cheese, green beans, and corn bread on the side makes his mouth water.

KG signals for the waitress.

"Good afternoon, KG," the waitress says.

"Let little man get whatever he want."

The waitress looks at David. He is blushing and is hiding the biggest smile ever behind the large menu.

While David is ordering, a short, muscular man who looks like he is in his mid 50s comes to the table. "Eh, KG."

KG stands up immediately and gives the man dap. "What's happening, Reese?"

The dap is much different.

David looks at the man and then looks at KG. For the first time with KG, David witnesses someone who is not scared of him. In fact, it is the other way around. This time, KG is giving him the ultimate respect.

"You remember when I used to bring you here when you were a youngin'?" the man asks.

"Yes, sir, I was about his age." KG says, pointing to David.

The man looks at David, studying his facial features.

"What's your name, son?" Reese asks.

"David."

David gets shy when the man is talking to him. He lowers his head.

"Look a man in his eyes when he's talking to you, David," KG says.

David looks up inch by inch until he finally connects with the man's light brown eyes.

"How old are you?"

"I'm eleven."

"Eleven, huh? You look familiar."

Reese begins to study David like an ancient artifact. "I know I have seen you somewhere," he says.

After a couple of seconds of talking to himself and shaking his head, a light bulb goes off.

"You're Gary's son."

David laughs.

KG looks surprised. "You mean Big G from the Parkside Projects?"

"No, my father's name is Thomas," David interrupts.

"No. I knew your father from back in the day. You look just like him. His son would be around your age."

KG raises an eyebrow. His eyes widen and his mouth slightly opens. All of a sudden David looks much different to him.

Reese gives KG a signal to not say anything else about it.

For the rest of the time they are there, David looks confused and KG keeps mumbling under his breath, "I can't believe you are Big G's son."

Daniel looks both ways before crossing the busy street, looks up to his Gramps's bedroom window and as soon as he swings James's car door open, the bass of Busta Rhymes's lyrics hit him like a thick cloud of smoke. He wrinkles his nose at the smell of old leather and cigar smoke and tries not to sit on the yellow padding gushing through the cracks of the seat.

"Can you turn the music down?" Daniel yells, reaching for the volume dial.

James smacks his hand down. He leans back, hand stretched to the steering wheel and says, "Just sit back and chill."

Daniel tries sitting back a little, but his seat is leaning so far into the backseat, he can't seem to get comfortable. His fingers fumble around for the lever until finally he gives up. He leans all the way back and tries mimicking Jason's cool look.

While cruising down the street, Daniel has to take in the abandoned buildings, empty store fronts with shattered windows, and playgrounds full of grown men instead of happy playful children. He finds it hard to believe that people live in such disparity.

"This is America, not Africa," he mumbles. He covers his mouth and glances at James.

James keeps his eye on the road. "It's different, huh?" He lets out a chuckle. "Just like Africa is not all poor and dirty, America is not all rich and virtuous."

Daniel's eyes narrow on the kids that are running around the hot concrete floor without shoes. It reminds him of the half-naked children on the commercial with bugs gnawing at their skin while they are on the ground scooping up rice and wandering in a field of trash to find food.

Daniel looks back over at James. He nods his head. *How could anyone be happy living here?*

As soon as they reach the tiny apartment, James heads straight to his room, leaving Daniel standing by the door as if he's holding it up. Daniel spots a man sitting on the couch. He also has tattoos everywhere, including black inked designs drawn all over his face. Daniel stands there at the door with his arms by his side, heart beating fast. He is afraid to sit down or open up his mouth to say hi, so he just allows his eyes to wander around the room.

The first thing that catches Daniel's eyes are the many obituaries lined up along the wall. The pictures of smiling faces with the words R.I.P. haunt him. He also sees a bronze looking picture of what he assumes to be James's parents. They too have digits for their birth and digits for the day they died. Daniel now wears an eerie look. *Why does he know so many people who have died? The only person I know who has died is my grandma.*

"What you looking at?" the man sitting on the couch asks.

Daniel doesn't answer. His face is blank, stance frozen.

The man turns to him with a hard look and says, "Come here."

Daniel rolls his eyes. *Not again.* He takes a silent deep breath, but moves toward the man anyway.

"Take off your shoes. I want 'em."

Just looking at the man's ink stained skin makes Daniel want to turn around and run. He reminds him of the men that his father locks up, and the men that his gramps always points out and talks about how ignorant and dangerous they are.

Daniel looks down at his shoes. He taps his white Reeboks around. He then looks back at the now impatient look on the man's face. Daniel shakes his head. He bends over, lifts his shoe up, pulls the shoe off of his heel, then off his foot.

I should just throw the shoe at him and run.

He reasons with the idea. He feels the man's eyes piercing his back as he bends down for his other shoe. It causes his hair to rise up on his arms. Shaking his head, Daniel stands on one foot and tugs his other shoe off.

He hears footsteps and sees a shadow coming closer to him. He looks up.

"Leave that boy alone," James says, shaking his head. He bends down and grabs Daniel's shoe.

Daniel watches as the men stare at him and laugh so loudly they have to hit the spine of the couch to let it all out.

"He just fucking with you," James says.

The man stops laughing. His sudden grim expression freaks Daniel out.

The man gets up and towers over Daniel.

"Don't ever walk in somebody's house without speaking and don't judge a man before they even open up their mouth. Ya momma ain't teach you that?"

With his head facing the man's chest, Daniel's eyes move up to the man's head. He nods.

"What did she teach you then?"

Daniel looks up to the ceiling.

"Nothing."

"All right."

The man puts his hand out to shake Daniel's hand.

He shakes it.

"My name is Roger. What's your name?"

"Daniel."

Roger gives Daniel a genuine smile. "Nice to meet you."

James is finally ready to go. He is carrying three large book bags and has changed into a neat button down and khaki shorts. Just looking at him, you wouldn't be able to tell that he has an inch of tattoo ink on him. His flip flops are jumping off of the floor and his hair is slicked down like he has just left prep school.

Daniel is wondering why he has changed his clothes.

"Come on. Let's get it," James says, opening the door.

Daniel heads out first, stopping at the Oldsmobile and grasping the door handle to open it.

"Naw. We over here," James says, walking toward a black, shiny Lexus.

Confused and appalled, Daniel walks over to the car.

The serenading sounds of classical music fill the air and instead of bending corners and driving reckless, James is taking his time as if he suddenly realizes life is short and he wants to slow down to enjoy every minute of it. They slow down at the entrance of a large brick building with a sign that reads, "College of Psychology." Daniel scans the landscape, the students rushing to class, and wonders why James of all people would be coming there.

"Good afternoon, Mr. Harris," a man with a thick grey beard says to James.

"How are you doing today?"

The students in the large classroom - much like an auditorium - disperse and hurry out of the building for their next class. James shakes hands with the professor and walks to the podium as Daniel sits down in a theatre-like folding chair. He waits quietly. He studies the two as they converse about the theoretical differences between Sigmund Freud and Carl Jung. The more he hears James speak, the more his words chip away at the perception of the man.

After a quick chat, James and Daniel head to the cafeteria. Daniel grabs a greasy burger with a handful of cold fries while James flirts with the smiling girls that are just about ready to drop their panties for the charismatic hottie.

"Hello, Professor Terry," James says.

The beautiful woman gives him a lingering smile and with a sweet yet authoritative voice says, "James. How are you?"

Daniel sucks in the last drops of his smoothie and the two head to the parking lot. While scanning the parking lot, Daniel spots the professor he had met not even an hour earlier pulling a plastic container, lifting it up, and then putting it in the trunk of his Jeep. He smiles at Daniel.

"You both have a nice day now," the professor says with a wide grin and a wave of his hand.

Daniel waves back, but not before noticing something. He looks around for the bags that he and James carried in. They are gone. As he is about to blurt out, "We forgot the bags," James gives him a look. Slung around James' shoulder is one of the bags. *But where's the other?*

Once they arrive back to the house, James and Daniel jump out of the Lexus and back into the Oldsmobile. He looks back at the Lexus as James turns the corner and sees Roger, his tattooed friend, get into the car. He glances back at James with so many questions swimming in his mind, he can't think straight.

James smiles back at Daniel. "I saw this cutie today when I was waiting on you to come out," he says. "I called her to come here, but the damn gate. It look bad to be on the other side of the gate. You feel me?"

Daniel sits up and nods his head. His expression is blank as he scrambles to find a way to answer.

"If I can just get through the gate, I'd probably be able to find her," Jason says slowing down for a red light. "Man, she was fly as hell."

Daniel's feet tap the carpet with excitement. He looks at James with a wide smile. "I can get you the passcode," he blurts out.

James instantly shakes his head. "Naw, it's not that deep."

"No really! I can get the passcode and then you can come in. Then you won't have to wait for me from out the gate."

James smiles at Daniel and Daniel smiles back.

"I can get it," Daniel reassures him.

Daniel is more pumped up than ever. Feeling like a hero that just saved the day, he starts to move his head and hands to the rhythm of the song. The loud sounds are now stimulating him as he allows it to relax his stiff body.

James looks at him and says, "Cool. I knew this was going to be a slick ass summer."

CHAPTER THIRTEEN

In the barely lit auditorium, Sam listens to the director of the "It Takes a Village" Program. "Now I know that sitting on that bus for twelve hours coming all the way to North Carolina University was probably a lot. But remember the reason why you are here. We are here so that you can be exposed to the many opportunities offered to you in life."

It gets quiet in the auditorium. Sitting beside Amina, Sam opens up her book bag and hands her a piece of paper.

Amina looks back at Sam and smiles. "So I see you did your homework, huh?"

"Yep," Sam proudly says.

Amina unfolds the loose leaf paper and flattens it with the palm of her hands. Holding it up a couple of inches away from her bronze, rectangular eyeglasses and then smoothing her hair down on the side from her face, she starts reading it. All that Sam can see are Amina's stubby, painted fingernails and the silhouette of her small, round head.

As Amina travels from line to line, her eyes begin to take in every word, throwing her into the life of Sam.

My name is Samantha Lariyah Johnson. What are my dreams? What do I want out of life? I want to be rich. If I was rich I could move out of my mother's house and take care of myself. I won't have to worry about locking my bedroom door. There are so many bad people trying to come in. I can shop for food when I get hungry.

If I had money, I could take my stepmother to one of those special places that help addicts. She needs help too. I want a mother too. I want a mother like the kids at school have. They have mothers that hug them. They have mothers that play with their hair and scream in the stands like they are their best friends. I take that back. If I had a lot of money, I could have saved my mother from dying. She would have been able to pay the money she needed so that she could have had surgery. I don't want my new mom. I just want my old one.

What do I think is stopping me?

I have no money. How am I going to be rich one day if I live in a place where only kids from rich parents can get rich? I see them excited about going to college with no worries. I see them riding in their nice cars talking about what new car they are going to get for their birthday. I see them. But they cannot see me. No one I know ever goes to college. No one I know ever gets rich. I guess that's why they call it a dream. I never get to wake up. I've had so many dreams. None ever come true. I can never get what I want. Not someone like me.

Amina holds the paper longer than she has to. Even though she has already read the letter, she feels the need to gather her thoughts before allowing any words to part from her mouth.

What came to mind as Amina read the letter were the many letters she had received from the more privileged children, the students she tutored in affluent neighborhoods. Their letters were much different. It cut to the chase: "I am going be an engineer like my aunt. My father is teaching me how to run the family business. My biggest fear is letting him down." Those kids don't even think about where their next meal will come from. They are not worried about bills. Their minds are free, unburdened. Their necessities are a given.

She then shakes her head at the lack of high expectations she sees in the inner city. "If only I had more support in helping these kids," she mumbles.

Amina lowers the paper down to her lap. She looks into Sam's eyes. It reminds her of how she herself was stuck on survival mode, waiting for someone to come along and reset her settings, her mindset, heighten her expectations.

Amina fights back her tears. She swallows deeply. Instead of shedding a tear, Amina's voice thickens with attitude. "Let me tell you something. It doesn't matter where you come from, who your mother is, who your father is, or how many people try to tell you that you are not good enough. You are only as intelligent as you think you are. If you really believe…"

Amina pauses.

"It's a rat. A rat!" Amina shouts out. Immediately, everyone in the auditorium turns their head, including Sam. An old woman with a cane almost breaks her neck to get down the aisle. Sam's feet are up by her chest as she watches people jump from their seats and head to the exit. The director comes running over.

"What's wrong? What happened?" she asks.

"My apologies, I thought I saw something," Amina says with a smile and a nod.

Amina sits back down while the director walks away shaking her head.

"Did you see that?" Amina says. "If you really believe that there is a rat, a fire or anything dangerous, you will run. Even if there is no danger, you will run. Once you run, everyone else will start to believe you because you are taking action. It might take a while for people to follow you, support you, because maybe they are a bit slow. Maybe they have experienced false alarms, so it takes them a while to get past their own doubts, but you keep going. Eventually, you will have the whole building behind you. If you truly believe in something, just go do it. But you have to believe it. You can't sit here and tell me one thing, try to sell me a dream, go back home, and sit on the couch and do nothing. That's not someone who believes. That is someone who dreams. Now, what are you going to do about your situation?"

Amina pokes Sam in the shoulder. Sam jerks away, laughing. "How are you going to use the resources that we provide to get you into college or get you into doing something you love to do?"

Sam shrugs her shoulders.

Amina places a piece of paper in Sam's hand and plops a pen down on it too.

"You said you wanted to be a professor, right?"

Sam nods her head.

Amina points to a tall man sitting in the corner. His legs are crossed with his nose in a book. He is waiting for the speakers to show up, too.

"Take this opportunity to go over there and ask that man as many questions as possible. Ask him about his struggles; ask him about his schedule; ask him about some books he recommends you read. Take notes, now. Because tonight, while everyone is sleeping…"

Sam cuts her sentence off and finishes it, "While everyone is sleeping, while everyone is playing video games and up talking, I will be working toward my goals."

"Exactly," Amina says with a proud smile.

In Cherry Hills, Florida, Daniel is now having the time of his life. He enjoys hanging out with James and Roger, his big brothers, and being taught special skills along the way. But it's almost time for him to go back home. His big brother James has schooled him on everything - everything except one important skill: girls.

"You got a girlfriend?" James asks with a mouth full of orange chicken.

Attempting to hide his embarrassment, Daniel grinds the plastic straw between his back teeth. "No."

"Well. I'm about to show you how to get one. First I'mma hook you up with some new clothes. You ain't going to catch no cuties with loafers and a whack ass baseball cap on your head."

He looks over Daniel's clothes and shakes his head. "You're going to have to stop letting your mother pick out your clothes." James lets out a chuckle. "Girls like bad boys, remember that."

James pushes his plate of Chinese food to the side and leans in to Daniel.

"You have to be a bad boy. Be too nice and they will disrespect you. Be too aggressive or thirsty, and they will ignore you. Find a median and they will do whatever you want them to do."

James scans the mall. He spots a young girl with short shorts on, a thin tank top, and sandals. "That's ya girl right there. Go holla at her."

In a nearby seat, James sits down and watches Daniel's hands shake as he approaches his first girl.

"Hello," he says to the short girl with a timid voice.

"Hi," she says, walking right past him.

Daniel looks back at James, who is waving for him to follow her, makes a muscle to tell him to take charge, and sits up straight to show him to walk with confidence.

James laughs as Daniel jerks his back up and down like a robot in an attempt to copy.

"I... I..."

By the time Daniel can get a word out, the girl cuts the corner and is gone.

For the rest of the day, Daniel works on walking up to girls while James falls back and watches. James laughs at moments, but ultimately feels proud to help the boy get a couple of numbers.

"I'll see you tomorrow. Same time, Dan," James shouts from his car window.

"Fo sho," Daniel yells back.

James drops Daniel off at the gate. But before walking home, Daniel's dry mouth and need for some cool air motivates him to go into the Cherry Hill Community Center before walking to his gramps' condo.

"I can't wait to see Rhonda," he says, thinking about the community director's welcoming smile. "Maybe she can take me 'sightseeing' around the neighborhood like last time."

He looks at the golf cart parked in front of the building. "Yeah, that was fun. Or maybe she made some chocolate chip cookies again."

Daniel walks into the building, allowing the cold rush of air to hit him in the face. He bends down to take a drink from the cold flowing water and hears a woman with a soft voice talking. *That must be Rhonda.*

"I am going to need you to be a little bit more observant," Rhonda says. "The residents are starting to look for another place to live. One woman just packed up her bags and left her condo without even putting it on the market first," Rhonda says.

Daniel lets the water run, but his ears are taking in everything she is saying. He then hears his buddy Greg, the security guard, who also adores and looks out for him.

"I know. I am trying my best. The cameras are just not catching any good footage. I really don't know what else to do, but–"

Rhonda interrupts. "Well, you need to try damn harder."

Daniel hears their voices getting closer. In a hurry, he presses the push button on the water fountain in and dips his head back down toward the water. The water is hitting his lips, but not a drop is making it into his mouth.

"Oh, I didn't see you there," Rhonda says with a high pitched friendly tone.

"I was just getting some water. I'm leaving," Daniel says, rushing out of the door and running toward his grandfather's condo.

Daniel gets to the doorstep and sees a paper rolled up into a tube sitting on his gramps' welcome mat.

Curious, he sits his bag of candy down on the dusty mat, pulls off the rubber band, and reads the paper.

Attention Great Residents of Cherry Hill. There has been a series of break-ins and robberies in the area and we need your assistance. As you might already know, Mrs. Carter has been the latest victim of a robbery. At approximately one o'clock Saturday afternoon, she was walking to her car and was assaulted by three masked men. One of the perpetrators struck her in the head with what is believed to have been a brick and she is currently in critical condition at a nearby hospital. It is believed that the robbers have in their possession a pearl necklace, a three carat diamond ring (Princess Cut) and a Rolex watch. This is just one of a series of crimes that has been committed over the summer. If you have any information, it is extremely important that you contact the police. We also have a list of crimes available at our office. We have added three more security officers to our team and are adding additional cameras. Please remain vigilant, but also know that we are doing everything in our power to keep our neighborhood safe.

Daniel takes the paper inside along with his bag of candy.

"Hey, Gramps."

"Hi, son. What you got there?"

"Just some Skittles and a couple of candy bars." He lifts the bag up in the air. "Oh, and a Coke."

"That's it?" His Gramps says. "Well if you want I can take you to the store so you won't have to keep going to the corner store every five minutes. All you have to do is ask."

Daniel smiles at his gramps.

"It's okay. My mother says I need the exercise."

"What's the piece of paper in your hand?"

Daniel's natural reaction was to lie, but then it only takes him a second to twist the situation.

"Just a notice saying that there have been a lot of crimes in the area lately and for us to watch our backs. Um, be careful. Probably just some niggers."

Gramps smiles. "You're probably right, son. You're probably right."

CHAPTER FOURTEEN

Summer vacation is ending, and Cathy is driving David back home for the last time. David's far from being happy about it.

With every stop sign and traffic light that gets him closer to home, his heart sinks lower and lower. Almost every week of his summer was spent either studying with Cathy or kicking it with KG. They were his escape from life at home, they were his family. He even tagged along at the family get-togethers and birthday parties. David was the boy that didn't look like the other family members, yet fit in so perfectly. Most of the time when he was with Cathy or KG, everyone referred to him as "Cuz."

Cathy tries to ignore David's silence as he watches the windshield wipers swipe away the falling rain, but it is hard. It isn't easy for her to say goodbye either.

"So, David. Are you excited about school?"

"No," David says with his tilted head resting on the door.

With every question she asks, he snaps back a quick yes or no.

When they finally pull up into the broken up driveway, Cathy puts the car into park and then rests her hand on David's shoulders.

"Looks like someone's getting a little muscle," she says, giving it a squeeze.

David can't help but laugh.

"Trying to look good for Sam, huh? That's something you can look forward to when you go back to school. You talked about her the whole summer."

David's smile goes limp again.

Thoughts of Sam make him feel good, but it also makes him sad. Deep down, he knows that Sam doesn't like him like that.

"Look, I'll come get you over Thanksgiving and Christmas break," Cathy says.

The words are a bit satisfying for David, but not quite good enough.

"Plus! I have a little surprise for you. You know your big brother wasn't going to let you go to school without a fresh outfit."

She reaches into the back seat and struggles to pull the two bulky bags from over the shoulders of the seats. "Come on. You can open them inside so your mom can see it, too. Let's hurry before it starts pouring out here."

Cathy and David walk into the house. Cathy breathes in the floral smell. Her eyes catch the beautifully decorated couch with the brightly colored pillows, but nothing can lighten or cover up the depressing feeling every time she enters the house.

"Wow, David. Look at that," Tara says.

David's frown breaks and forms into a smile. His eyes light up as Cathy is pulling out a pair of brand new shoes. They widen when he sees that they are a rare pair of Jordans. David remembers KG talking about them before they were released. He then remembers KG wearing them a couple of weeks later.

"Look, David. They are your favorite colors, too - black and red. Just like your father," Tara says excited.

David frowns.

"We're not done," Cathy says, pulling out a matching outfit.

David can't hold back any longer. He throws his arms around Cathy and squeezes her tight. He doesn't want to let go.

Tara looks at her son's joy and smiles. "Thank you so much, Cathy. You have been a blessing," Tara says almost in tears.

"We love him. He's never a problem," Cathy says.

As David watches Cathy pull away and disappear from his driveway, his mother rubs the side of his head.

"They must really love you, boy."

She looks at the huge bag of school supplies Cathy left behind and shakes her head.

"I am so happy you have what you need to start school."

Thomas walks from the back room after observing them from the end of the hallway.

"David, go clean your room. Now!" he says roughly.

David can feel the tension growing in the house already. It never fails. He rolls his eyes, just out of Thomas's view. He holds his head up high and then walks into his room.

Once in his room, he puts on his headphones and presses play on his CD player. He starts dancing, imitating the moves he saw KG do while dancing at a family cookout, then he starts mumbling the words to the song. Just the thought of going to school with a fresh outfit on makes him feel good. It's a new year and he is starting it off right, with a new outfit, new confidence, and just maybe with the chance of a new girlfriend, Sam. As he sweeps the trash into one big pile, he daydreams of walking into the classroom and catching everyone's attention.

He remembers everything that KG had taught him over the summer.

Some of his memories are embarrassing moments, while others are fascinating, but there is one special memory he will never forget. As he relives the memory, a feeling of joy comes over him.

"Damn, David, did you take a shower?" KG complained, smelling David's musty body.

"Yeah, a couple of days ago."

"A couple of days ago?" KG shouted out. "You blowing up my car."

David remembers KG swerving the car around and speeding back home. He gave David a face towel - the softest towel David had ever held - and a bath towel.

"Get in the shower and wash your ass. Wash your hair too. I'll be right back with some clothes for you. It'll only take me 10 minutes to run to the mall."

David did just that. He took a long hot shower. He scrubbed so hard, he could have scrubbed the brown tint off of his skin. He could tell the difference between the softness of the water and how it ran down his body. The bathroom was warm and the blue and white decor made it even more soothing. David got out of the bathroom and stepped onto the memory foam bath rug. His feet sank right in.

Just as promised, KG came back with a new outfit, shoes and all. "If you going to be rolling with me, you gotta be looking fly."

"Your clothes are by the door. Tell me when you get them on," KG yelled from behind the bathroom door.

A couple of minutes later, David walked out looking like a totally different boy. He felt different, too.

"Come here, little man." KG handed him some cologne and told him where to spray. He pulled out a brand new brush with bristles on both sides. "I want you to brush your head like this every day."

KG brushed each side of his head, from the top to the bottom.

David's head moved around as he tried to keep it in place.

While brushing his hair, KG continued talking to him.

"Every day when you look in the mirror, you should want to smile at yourself. Your reflection should make you say, 'Damn, I look good.' Go ahead and say it."

"I look good," David said with his head still moving with every stroke of the brush.

"That's not what I told you to say. Say, 'Damn, I look good.'"

David smiled. Hesitated, then said, "Damn, I look good."

KG laughed. "Now that's what I'm talking about."

KG dipped his hand into a jar that read "Ocean's Wave Grease."

He rubbed it on his head and then showed David how to wear a wave cap.

The memories of being with KG made David feel on top of the world. Even though he is cleaning his room and even though his father is an asshole, he now feels strong enough to handle his situation.

He then pauses to look out of his window. He sees a police car fly into the driveway and watches as Jacob comes storming out of the car and into his house. "What the...?" he heard Jacob say before slamming the front door so hard it shook the flowers hanging down from their porch.

"What the hell is this?" Jacob yells. He scans the messy house and then takes in a deep breath.

"So this is what I have to come home to after a month of training."

While Jacob is fanning the air and turning on every vent in the house and opening up doors, windows and spraying air freshener, the phone rings. It's his father.

"I think it's about time for me to move," his father rants. "This place is not suitable for me anymore. More and more, I see more black people moving in here, bringing all—"

Jacob shakes his head. "How is Daniel doing, Dad?"

"He is doing great. He has made a few friends in the neighborhood, so I barely see him."

There is a pause and then he continues. "I don't know. Ever since the weather broke, we have been having more and more reports of break-ins and car thefts. It's something about the weather that gets up in their skin."

"Dad, I have to go."

Jacob hangs up the phone. He is irritated about the shape of the house and also questioning whether or not Daniel should even spend another day with his father. He turns to the door and gives Sheri a cold stare as she comes walking in.

"What happened here? Where the hell have you been?" Jacob yells.

Jacob's face has turned bright red and he is fuming with anger.

Sheri just stands there, shocked and amazed at the way the house looks. She has bags in her hands from the grocery store. "Well, you came home early, I was going to prepare a nice dinner for you," she says in a high pitched soft tone.

"I hate when you do that. I hate when you act like everything is so fucking perfect." He waves his hand in the direction of the broken vase, the sink full of dishes and trash that's overflowing with beer cans and take-out boxes. Then he starts turning over the couch pillows.

"Here I am fighting to keep my job and you over here getting high with God knows who. The lights are off, the damn refrigerator is empty. What the hell are you doing, Sheri? My son will be here tomorrow. You want him to see this?"

The next day, David drags two large trash cans to the curb. He holds his breath to stop the wind from blowing the rancid smell into his face.

As he is turning around, he sees Daniel and an old man pulling up in a black, shiny Benz.

David waves at Daniel. Daniel doesn't wave back. *Well maybe he didn't see me,* David thinks to himself. He shrugs his shoulders and then continues up the driveway. Seconds later, Daniel gets out of the car. He grabs his Louis Vuitton bag out of the trunk and rolls it straight into the house, never uttering a word to David.

Daniel's grandfather gives David a quick look of disgust and then he too walks into the house.

"Oh, Daniel!" Sheri yells while hugging her son. "I've missed you."

Daniel gives her a weak hug.

Sheri leads him to his room to help unpack while Gramps and Jacob sit down and talk.

"I sure am going to miss him," Gramps says to Jacob.

Jacob looks worried.

"Why are you acting as if you're about to kick the bucket or something?"

"No," Gramps says, laughing. "I just really enjoyed him. I can't wait for him to come back. Maybe by then, I'll have moved out and away from those thugs. They seem to eventually follow me wherever I go anyway."

Jacob shakes his head and mumbles, "I wonder what all my son has been exposed to."

In Daniel's room, Sheri is gathering all of Daniel's dirty clothes. She wastes no time in putting them into his wicker laundry bin and then trucks them into the laundry room.

Starting off with his jeans, she checks the pockets, turns them inside out, and tosses them into the wide mouth of the washer. She does this to every pair, until she runs across a pocket that seems full. "Hmmmm. What is this?" she says.

She pulls out a wrinkled piece of paper and stops to read it. It is a list of crimes that occurred in Cherry Hill Estates over the past couple of months.

The list disturbs her, making her heart beat fast and her breaths become short. Around each crime, except for two, she sees a big smiley face drawn in pencil along with a set of initials written in red across it. *Well, that's awfully strange. Why would my little Daniel carry such a thing in his pocket?* For a second she thinks the worse. *Why else would my son be carrying this around?* But then she thinks about her son, his angelic smile and his soft voice. *Not my son. He couldn't possibly.*

CHAPTER FIFTEEN

David sprays on one last squirt of cologne given to him by KG and heads out the door to school. With his fresh waves and rocking his new exclusive Jordans, he feels good about his first day of school. Maybe it's the blue sky, the sun shining brightly above him or his new found confidence, but somehow he feels that today is going to be a good day.

"David, wait up!"

David glances back and sees Daniel running toward him. He rolls his eyes and sighs. *What the hell does he want?*

"David, my fault for dogging you the other day," Daniel says, exaggerating the need to catch his breath. "My gramps don't like black people. He a little off."

"So what that got to do with you?" asks David, pausing to look Daniel straight in the eyes.

Daniel is caught off guard by David's straightforward response.

"I don't know. I guess I felt a little embarrassed to…" He looks at David's hard look. "I'm sorry."

David looks at his old friend. The friend that used to come knocking at his door so they could jump on the trampoline; the friend that used to crack jokes with him on his porch and talk about football. Much like himself, Daniel has also changed over just the course of a summer.

Daniel is dressed similar to James, his summer mentor, rocking a pair of white and powder blue Air Force Ones, a hoodie and jeans. He looks at David, waiting for a response.

"What's up?" David asks, still disappointed.

"Nothin'. I just wanted to show you something. I came up on this while I was in Florida."

Daniel jerks his head back at the language Daniel is using. He mouths the words, "Came up?" *Since when does he talk like that?* He lets out a chuckle.

Interested in what Daniel has to show him, David stops by a tree and waits for him to unzip his book bag.

Daniel balances his book bag on one knee, dips his hand inside and turns his back toward the street. He pulls it out.

David narrows his eyes. Cupped in Daniel's hand is a ring. It is a small band with a huge diamond sitting on top of it. The edges sparkle in the sunlight.

"Where'd you get that from?" David asks.

"Florida."

"No shit," David says. "What you gon' do with it?"

"Sell it." Daniel snaps back.

David immediately turns around and starts walking off. He doesn't wait for Daniel to tuck the diamond back into his book bag. Instead he intentionally picks up his pace.

David looks back at his old friend and shakes his head. *KG told me about people like him. The people that smile in your face and then bite you in the back. Snakes.* David turns back around thinking about what KG had said. Then he thinks about the crack that Daniel had shown him months earlier. *He ain't nothin' but trouble.*

Daniel watches his friend walk away and he lets him. "My gramps told me about people like him." He narrows his eyes as David walks away. "Niggers."

In homeroom, David sits down in the very back of the class. His book bag is resting beside his shoes while he watches students one by one find a seat. He watches the new faces look for seats like lost puppies, and then he notices the familiar people who are already getting comfortable and cliquing up.

David smiles at the beautiful girls, especially the eighth graders. They have morphed. They are no longer wearing knee length skirts, showing their bony legs. They are now pushing the limits with tight skirts and thin t-shirts that are squeezing their budding breasts, and tights that do nothing but accent the maturing shape of their legs.

More and more students trickle into the crowded classroom, some looking much different than the last time he saw them with their pimples and budding facial hair, while others just look different with a new haircut. A lot of things have changed. But there is one thing that he has realized has stayed the same. Yet again, students pass him by. They laugh, joke, and talk around him as if he is not there. Yet again, he is invisible. No one sees the boy who has spent hours brushing his hair, brushing his teeth until his gums are almost pink, or the twenty-two sprays of cologne he used to saturate his whole body, including every inch of his outfit. No one notices.

He sits there and tries to convince himself that he doesn't care. *I ain't do this for them anyway. The only person that I care about is Sam. If I can just see Sam, I'm cool,* David thinks while watching the teacher draw symbols on the chalkboard.

Class after class, there's no sign of Sam. No chance of getting the least bit of attention from anyone.

"Same thing. Nothing has changed," he says walking through the school hallways. A daunting feeling takes over him as he hears the last bell ring signaling the end of the school day.

Where is she? I didn't even get a chance to show her my new outfit. He looks down at his Jordans, his white t-shirt with Jordan frozen in mid air ready to dunk, and shakes his head. *Maybe I can wear it tomorrow.* He shakes the idea from his thoughts. *I can't do that. That's not cool.* He sighs, his head lowers and his once confident walk down the courtyard is now more like a drag.

Determined to see Sam, David stands in the middle of the schoolyard. As the kids in the school pass him by, some almost knocking him down, he wonders if he really is invisible.

"Eh, David," a tall, light-skinned boy yells from behind him. "Nice shoes."

David turns his head to the sound. *About damn time somebody noticed my shoes.* He almost cracks a smile. But then when he sees whose voice it is, he wonders if instead of smiling, he should run.

David looks up at Dashawn, the biggest bully at Garrison Heights Middle School. He has beaten up every dude that thought they could fight. He has been suspended countless times, but his parents practically own the city. Therefore, it would not be in the best interest of the school to totally suspend him. They just put up with him. And along with Dashawn comes an entourage of wanna-be thugs, following him around like he is feeding their families.

"What size are those, man? Those are some hard ass Jordans," Dashawn says walking up on David.

David looks down at his feet, attempting to check them out himself. He glances down for only a second. By the time he looks back up, he sees the boys huddling around him. So much so that he can't see anything other than jerseys, t-shirts, and hoodies. It seems as if the school yard has disappeared, just big, heavy breathing boys, some with dragon breath and others who look like they have just walked off the set of a gangster movie.

"Give me the shoes," Dashawn commands.

"No! I ain't giving you shit," David yells back. His heart speeds up, but he lifts his chest out even more. Thinking about what KG might do, he mimics his mentor's confidence.

Dashawn gets right up in David's face. His chest is just an inch from David's and he is staring down at him as if he is ready for whatever.

"Get up off of me," David says, pushing him away, only managing to move him an inch or two.

Dashawn steps back. With great momentum, he lunges forward, connects his balled fist to David's right cheek bone and punches him with so much strength it knocks him down to the concrete.

David feels his face go numb. The world is spinning as the bright blue sky gets lighter and lighter. He can also feel a tugging at his feet. Dashawn yanks his feet so hard he is pulled with his shoe. Suddenly, each foot falls to the concrete with only a sock to protect the impact of his shoe slamming to the ground.

Within mere seconds, they are gone.

"David! David!"

David hears a voice getting closer and closer to him. He opens his eyes. They struggle for a while to focus, but soon he is able to make out the face that is moving around him. The face goes from a blurry blob to the beautiful face of Sam. David almost smiles.

He sits up. He looks at his white socks and then he looks at Sam.

Sam is almost unrecognizable. She is wearing a pink t-shirt with a jean romper, her once wavy hair is now straight and seems as if it has grown some inches, and she is much taller now.

"You ok?"

"Yeah. I'm good."

David gets up, dusts himself off, trying to act like he is all right, and then walks off.

"What's wrong with you, David?" Sam shouts, arms folded and shaking her head.

David looks back at her. "What does it look like? I ain't got no shoes," he yells, throwing up his hands.

Sam looks back at him. She has to bite her tongue. "Fine then, just leave," she mumbles.

David walks home by himself. He doesn't want to be around anyone. All he can think about is how messed up his life is. He drags his feet up his steps and enters his front door, slamming the screen behind him. Immediately he hears his father.

"David, go to the store and get me a Black."

David rolls his eyes and nods his head.

"I need the money," David yells back.

"It's on the counter."

David grabs his old pair of Reeboks and walks to the store. While walking through the parking lot of his old neighborhood, he sees an old friend from East Mount Elementary.

"What's up?" the boy says, hanging out of the window of a pickup truck.

David nods his head to him, but keeps walking into the store. "Oh, you acting like you too good fa us, huh? Acting all white and shit, now that you live in the heights, huh?" the boy taunts. "Look at you with them old ass Reeboks. You still look beat up. Still ain't got shit."

Full of frustration, David swings the door open, and walks in shaking his head. *I can't win.* He sighs. Once inside, David grabs a twenty-five cent zebra cake and a twenty-five cent red soda and slams it on the counter.

"Whats up, D?" the cashier asks.

David gives him a look, then two nods.

The cashier looks back at him, grabs two Black and Mild shells, and slyly plops them into the bag.

"You got it?"

"Yeah," David says, walking back into the house.

David throws the shell to his father, who is sitting in the living room watching TV, and then heads to the back. He locks his door. He thinks about his shoes, his life and his luck. *Why do bad things always happen to me? I don't even be doing shit.*

David opens the plastic wrapper and pulls out the Black and Mild. With both hands, he rubs the stick in between his hands like it's a genie bottle and watches as the brown mystery particles fall into a piece of paper on his lap. Once all of the contents are gone, he pulls out the brown paper and carefully repacks the shell - making sure not to leave any residue behind. Inhaling the burning stick gives him an instant rush - making his head spin. A good head spin. It relaxes his mind and his muscles.

Weeks and then months pass and it seems like lost time to David. He comes to school late almost every day, he spends most of his classroom time lying down on the desk, and his teachers are still passing him. They stopped calling the house since it doesn't make a difference.

Every day when David gets home, he does the same thing. Nothing. He doesn't even own a book bag anymore. He sold it for a fake gold chain.

Deep down inside he knows he can do better, especially since he sees how much Sam has blossomed into a smart and driven young girl.

"Ms. Amina!" Sam says, spinning through the library's revolving door.

"Sam! What's going on? You're here early. The students haven't even arrived yet," Amina says.

"I know. I know." Out of breath, Sam drops her heavy book bag on the floor. She fans the paper in the air for Amina to take it.

"Well, what is this?" Amina carefully pulls the paper out of the envelope. Sam watches her intently.

Suddenly, Amina's eyes widen.

"Whoa, straight A's again. And you only have one more semester to go."

Amina narrows her eyes at Sam. "Whose report card did you steal?"

Sam laughs and then gives Amina a hug. "Thank you, Amina. Thank you."

Once Sam finishes tutoring her last student, she goes home and decides to finally hang up a poster she had made with Amina over the summer. She grabs the wide poster board and holds it up into the air. Right in front of her are her dreams. And for the first time in her life, she actually believes it's possible.

The first picture she looks at is a picture of college students. Some are wearing jerseys with big bright letters on the back reading, "Ohio State," while others are wearing jeans and red and white t-shirts with college books in their hands. They are all walking to a huge stone building. She reads the words softly to herself, "College of Education."

Then there are other pictures, like her dream car, the Range Rover, and a huge mansion sitting on top of a hill.

"Yep, that's gonna be me," she brags.

She hangs the posters up right beside her bookshelf. Then she steps back to look at her wall of achievements and dreams. Her bookshelf is her favorite. Just looking at the rows and rows of books she has collected and read makes her feel proud. Her eyes fall on her mother's journal. *I swear if I could just find the other journals,* she thinks. For a second she marinates on the thought of looking for them again, but then gives up on the idea.

I guess I will write in my own journal for now. She grabs the notebook she started writing in over the summer. Then rereads the note Amina had written in the flap. "Create your own environment by filling your mind with books, by surrounding yourself with positive people. Focus on your dreams and blur out everything and everybody else. Then and only then will you, Samantha Johnson, become great. I love you. *Amina G.*"

CHAPTER SIXTEEN

It's one week before Christmas break and the streets are filled with snow and the houses are covered with blinking rainbow colored light bulbs.

Through a kitchen window, David is watching a boy and his father throw snowballs at each other. The little boy cocks his arm back and flings the small ball toward his father. His father dodges it and then chases him through the yard. *Must be nice*, David thinks to himself while focusing on the laughter and joy coming from the two.

David looks over at Thomas. He is sitting down on the couch watching Maury. "I slept with my baby's father's father."

David watches him prop his legs on the couch and it angers him.

It pisses him off just watching him toss up the Budweiser bottle and yell at the TV.

"Man, I swear," Thomas says. "If Tara ever did some slick shit like that to me, I'd kill her."

David's eyes squint so tight he can barely see Thomas. He gets up from the chair, grabs a knife from the drawer, and tightens his grip around it.

"If anyone is going to get killed, it's your lazy ass," David mumbles to himself. He drops the knife back into the drawer.

"What? What you say, boy?" Thomas says, cutting his eyes at David.

David just stands there. He stands tall, stares back at his father, and then turns around to the refrigerator to gather himself.

Thomas gets off the couch, each leg calmly hitting the floor. He rises up like a tall tree and walks toward David, never breaking the cold stare.

"What did you say to me?" His voice is rough and intimidating.

Thomas steps head to head with David, towering over him, so close in fact, that David can feel the heat of his breath against his cheek.

David takes a step back, and then turns around, but not before mumbling another set of words to himself.

Thomas lunges at David, grabbing the back of his shirt. With great strength he yanks him down to the floor. David's legs fly up in the air as he lands hard on his back. David is caught off guard. He throws his hands up, as if to surrender, but it is much too late.

Thomas grabs him by the neck, covering every inch of it.

"What you gon' say now, huh?" he whispers in his ear while lifting David's head and slamming it back down to the floor. Thomas's eyes grow large, almost popping out of their sockets.

David is speechless, taking each blow to the head like a champ. He tries fighting back, using his forearms to push Thomas off of him, then hitting him in the face, but his strength leaves his body.

David can't breathe. He starts to move wildly, trying to set himself free.

Thomas looks at him and smiles. He loosens his grip, just enough for David to take in air, something he values more than anything now.

"Mumble if you want to. It'll be your life."

Thomas gets up and walks back to the couch.

David is left in the middle of the dining room floor, breathing in and out deeply, feeling weak and powerless. Tears roll down the side of his face. He takes a deep swallow to refresh his dry throat and shakes his head. *I hate him. I swear I'mma kill'im.*

The next day, David gets up and goes to school as usual. Sitting in class, he does the same thing, nothing.

"David," Mrs. Calloway calls. The other kids in the class turn toward David. Some snicker while others show sympathy for him.

"David!" Mrs. Calloway repeats.

He doesn't move. He is staring at his desk.

"David!" she yells, becoming frustrated.

A boy sitting next to David scoots his chair over. He watches David dig his pencil into the wooden desk as if he's possessed, not blinking an eye.

Mrs. Calloway's heart drops. She is getting goosebumps by the sudden change of behavior from the quietest and calmest student in the class.

"Stay after class," she tells him while walking back up to the front of the room.

After class, she tries talking to David. He never raises his head, never opens his mouth.

The next day of school, Mrs. Calloway catches David again not paying attention. This time, he is drawing circles on the desk.

"Mr. Peterson," she yells.

David ignores her. He refuses to look up to acknowledge her.

She walks over to him, folds her arms, and says, "What is the problem?"

David doesn't answer.

"Do I have to call your parents?"

Still no answer.

She notices tears falling onto his desk.

Concerned, she kneels down and with much effort lifts his face up to look deeply into his eyes.

His head rises, but his eyes remain focused on his desk. He's biting his lip, and she can see his chest rising and falling through his shirt.

Mrs. Calloway gently grabs David's free hand and walks him to the office. It is a touch that is so warm to him, something he has been longing for. She sits him down and tells the secretary that he needs to see the counselor.

While sitting in the warm room, David's eyelids overflow with tears. They are flowing out like a stream and he is allowing them to roam as freely as they please.

Everyone that passes him looks at him, but no one stops to comfort him. Then, from the corner of his eyes, David sees a man appear.

"And what do we have here?" the short muscular man says while wearing a gentle smile.

The secretary immediately drops her phone to address the principal. "Mrs. Calloway brought him here to talk to the counselor," she says.

"Come on back to my office," the principal says, waving his hand to David.

David gets up from the chair like it is the hardest thing for him to do. He drags his feet to the office - a small room with boxes still unpacked and pictures sitting on the floor waiting to be hung up. There is also a plastic sign with the words, "Mr. Harrington, Principal." It's sitting flat on the desk, waiting to be placed in its holder.

"Find a seat. Any seat."

David sits in a chair that is directly facing the principal and looks him dead in the eyes. David doesn't turn away. He doesn't blink. There is still tears coming down his face and his hands are balled up. He looks like he is ready to explode.

"Calm down. What is the problem? Why are you so angry?" Mr. Harrington says, leaning in toward David.

The words cause even more tears to fall, but David never flinches.

"My name is Ronnie. Ronnie Harrington. What's your name?" the principal asks.

David looks at him. The man he saw for the first time the other day as he joined the kids in a game of basketball, the man who gave each kid a high five at lunch, Mr. Harrington's demeanor and genuine concern make David comfortable.

David looks up at the man, hoping this time an adult will listen to him. "David," he mumbles.

"Now we are getting somewhere. David, can you tell me your last name?"

"Peterson."

"Peterson?"

Mr. Harrington's head tilts up, as if he is trying to retrieve a memory. It takes a second. Then he looks back at David. He tilts his head again.

"What's your mother's name?"

David mumbles, "Tara."

Mr. Harrington shakes his head. He is in disbelief. This time when looking at David, an overwhelming feeling comes over him. He now has a connection with this little boy. He is now feeling an urgent need to help him.

"I knew your father," he says. "We were best friends in high school."

Once again David is confused, but he doesn't say a word. He just sits there. There is no need to argue about who his father is. He knows it must be true.

Still angry, David just sits in the leather brown chair and stares at the man.

"Do you think you can sit here for the rest of the period? I am going to have the secretary call your mother. I really need to talk to her." In a hurry, Mr. Harrington lifts from his chair and leaves his office.

With his head resting on the cherry wood desk, and a jacket covering his head, David thinks about who his real father could be.

Why did my mother lie to me like that?

He daydreams. Like watching a movie, David sees himself walk into his mother's room, lift up the mattress, and grab the gun. He looks at it in his mind, waving the weight from side to side. He points it at himself. *Death has to be better than this.* He holds the gun up to his head for a second, and then he drops it down to his side. He stands there in the doorway until Thomas walks in. Lifting the gun up to Thomas's head, he points it at him and rubs the trigger.

Once again, the daydream ends with tears. However, the more David imagines it, the more confidence he has in himself that he can do it.

The office door clicks open. It's Mr. Harrington.

"I have talked to your mother," Mr. Harrington says, reassuring David that everything will be fine.

"I have plans to meet up with her. There are some things we must talk about concerning your welfare."

CHAPTER SEVENTEEN

Sitting at a nearby diner, Tara and Mr. Harrington discuss the issues surrounding David.

"Tara, what the fuck are you doing?" Mr. Harrington yells.

Tara looks down at the white tablecloth and shakes her head.

"Look at you. Look at your son. If Greg were here, you know like I know, you wouldn't be living like this. And his son?"

Tara bursts out into an uncontrollable sob. "I know. I know," she says getting louder and louder.

While Tara is crying and covering her face with embarrassment, Ronnie thinks about the last time he spoke to Greg. He remembers it clear as day.

"What's up, G?" Ronnie said, holding the phone close to his ear.

Greg's voice was different. He could tell something was wrong.

"I think I done fucked up. I really think I done fucked up big time," Greg said.

Ronnie drops his pencil and it falls in between the pages of his thick psychology book. He takes his eyeglasses off and then waits for an answer.

"Look, the reason why I called was because you the only one I can trust. If anything happens to me, I need you to take care of Junior."

"Fo sho, what's the problem?" Ronnie asked.

There was silence, heavy breathing, and then a long pause. "I wish I would have took your route. I wish I could have been as smart as you and got the fuck out of these streets. I don't think I'mma make it, man. I messed up…"

Ronnie's heart beat fast. He was speechless.

"Take care of li'l man, Ronnie. Take care of my li'l man."

Those were the last words that Ronnie heard from his best friend.

Just the guilt alone makes him almost want to ball up and cry. He reneged on his promise. Ronnie calms down. His words slow down and his voice softens. "I promised him I would take care of your son and I didn't. Now I am. Tell me the problem. Tell me why the hell you would go messing around with some corny dude that whoops your ass…and Greg's son?"

He pauses, swallows and shakes his head again. The thought of what Greg would do to Thomas if he were still alive makes him shiver. The pressure to do something weighs down on him. Here he is finally achieving his dream of becoming a principal, something he worked so hard for, and now he is sitting in front of his best friend's girl contemplating on killing her boyfriend.

Ronnie moves Tara's hands from her face and looks into her bloodshot eyes. "I'm going to drop you off and—"

Tara shakes her head nervously. "No, please, don't drop me off, he'll…"

Ronnie looks at her in disbelief. It is like he is in a dream - a nightmare. He had never seen Tara so weak. The last time he saw Tara, she was walking around with a big belly, the baddest outfit on, and gold around almost every finger of her hand. Greg took care of her, loved her, would have never hit her. Ronnie takes another deep breath.

Sitting on the porch at home, David is wracking his brain to figure out what is going on. *Who is my father?*

He is sitting on the last step in the dark under the moonlight sky, watching the stars, and then suddenly, he sees a figure. He gets anxious. Hoping that it's his mother, he jumps up.

"Damn, it's Dad. I mean Thomas."

Thomas walks right through the front door, almost pushing David out of the way. "Where's your mother?"

"I don't know."

Inside, David can hear Thomas's footsteps walking through every inch of the house.

"I told him she ain't here," David mumbles, shaking his head. David can sense the anger.

Ready to get out of the house and frustrated that he can't figure things out himself, he picks up the phone.

"Who is this?" KG asks.

"It's David."

"Oh. What's up, D?"

"I need you to pick me up."

"What's up?"

It's the first time David has ever called KG directly.

"I just need you to pick me up."

"Aight, I'm on my way."

In the middle of a fade, KG hops out of the chair, grabs his pager from the counter and yells back at the barber, "I gotta go."

"But. I…" The barber doesn't have time to finish his sentence. KG is already up the steps.

"Cut me up later. I gotta go."

He jumps in the car. Once the car starts up, the stereo automatically bangs Styles P's "I get high." He speeds out of the driveway. KG turns down the music to a low hum and then he takes his gun out of his holster and puts it into the glove compartment.

David gets up and walks into his father's back room. He sees him there staring at the TV, in a trance.

"I gotta go get a book from Sam's house. I left mine at school."

Thomas doesn't look away from the TV, he just continues to stare.

"Mmmm," is all he says.

David feels an uneasy feeling about Thomas. Something just doesn't feel right. The feeling stops him, makes him ponder whether he should leave the house or not. However, the thought only lasts for a couple of seconds because once he looks out the window and sees KG pull up, the feeling disappears. He needs to go. He needs to get some answers.

"Tara. Tara," Ronnie says, snapping at the sobbing woman. "What do you want me to do? What do you want me to do about this dude?"

"Nothing. I don't want you to do anything. I love him!"

Ronnie gets the urge to slap Tara right there in the Mexican restaurant.

He dips his head in close to her and whispers. "You've got to be fucking kidding me. This punk punches you, he slaps you, spits on you, and you still love him? You're crazy. You got your son out here looking like the son of a junkie. You out here looking like the walking dead and you up here talking about you love this dude. What happened to all that money Greg stashed away for you?"

Tara shrugs her shoulders.

"Tara!"

"So what's up, David? What's the problem?" KG asks while driving back to his house.

David looks at KG straight in his eyes. "I need to know who my father is. I need to know. Now!"

David can't even finish his words before tears start covering his face and mucous begins to coat his throat, making it harder for him to form his words.

Scurrr! KG slams on the brakes.

The car stops right in the middle of traffic. Cars are beeping their horns, tires are screeching, and foul words are being thrown at the car.

"What the fuck is going on?"

David had never talked to anyone about Thomas, and he didn't want to start, especially to KG. He knows KG will kill him. He chooses his words carefully.

David wipes his tears in a hurry and sucks up the snot in his throat, clearing air and allowing words to come out smoothly. The first thing that comes trembling out of his mouth is the first image that comes to mind.

"They took my shoes."

KG relaxes, his blood pressure descends, and he puts the car back into drive.

"I thought that man was hitting on you or something. You had me scared for a minute. Shoes. That's an easy fix. All you need to do is grow some balls. That's all. You grow some balls, you'll get your shoes back."

KG turns up the music, reclines back in his seat, and cruises back to the house.

"Tara, I am going to drop you off wherever you want me to drop you off, and then I am going to go home and think about what I am going to do next. I am not going to let David get hurt anymore. You best believe that," Ronnie says.

Ronnie does as promised. He drives Tara to the end of her street and lets her out. She opens the door, gets out, and then ducks into the car to tell Ronnie thank you. He nods to her and he takes off.

She walks with her head down trying to figure out what it is she is going to tell Thomas. Why was she coming home late? Why hasn't she cleaned or cooked him a meal? Why didn't she tell him where she was and who she was with?

The walk to her house is short. She has to come up with something fast. She has to figure out a good lie and be able to practice how she is going to say it or she knows that she will be getting a beating tonight.

She is so busy thinking, so busy tugging her clothes straight and patting her hair back together that she missed one important thing. She never looked back. She never looked around when she got out of the car. She knows to do that. She knows that Thomas always has his eyes on her.

Not far behind her, Thomas is walking. He is carrying a brown paper bag with a bottle of liquor in it. His fingers are gripping the neck of the bottle like it is Tara's neck. He is swinging with such strength that if released, it is sure to fly up and crack her in the head. He doesn't do it, though. He just walks and watches. He knows better than to start something in Garrison Heights. In the hood, it will take the police thirty minutes to show up and he could do a lot of damage in thirty minutes, but not in the suburbs. Two minutes flat and he'd be in jail.

His pace slows down as she walks up on the porch. He watches her take a deep breath, fix her hair, and wiggle out her nerves. Then she walks into the house.

In the basement, KG makes David stand up with his guards up and dance around the room. The poor barber sits in the chair watching. He wants to go home, but he knows not to say anything. He has to wait.

Dancing around like a young Muhammad Ali and punching the air, KG starts talking to David. "You want to know who your daddy is, huh?"

David looks at KG. He's no longer friendly. Instead he looks like he is about to swing on David. His hands are up and he is moving his feet so fast, it makes David nervous.

With a little force behind his arm, he punches David in the chest.

David falls to the ground. It is not the punch that causes the fall, but more of a surrender.

"Get back up, now. Get back up," KG yells.

David doesn't like this version of KG. He wants him to be nice to him. But being nice is the farthest thing on KG's mind. David gets back up slowly, only to be met with another punch deep into his chest.

"Your father. He was a boxer. The best in the state." KG lands another punch, but this time digging his knuckle into his arm. "Your father. He was a hustler. But not just any hustler. He pulled mad weight." KG punches David again. "Put your hands up now. Stop grabbing your arm. It ain't going nowhere." He punches him right where David is grabbing.

"His name was G. Then when he took over the East Side, they called him Big G. Your father wasn't a sucka and everybody knew it."

KG two pieces David so hard, David wants to cry.

"Are you gonna swing, or are you gonna keep taking my punches? Swing! Swing!" KG yells, egging him on.

David wipes the tears from his eyes and then throws a weak punch at the air.

"Who you tryna hit with that weak ass punch?"

All of a sudden, Cathy comes walking into the room.

David looks at her with a sigh of relief. *Maybe she'll stop him.*

She doesn't. She just smiles instead. She stands there, leans against the panel of the door with folded arms and watches.

David lifts his head. He suddenly realizes what is going on. KG didn't bring him down to the basement to beat him up. He brought him down there to teach him.

David's confidence jumps and all of a sudden he can remember a man teaching him to put his guards up. He can't remember how old he was, but he can remember how the man would slap his arms down and force him to put them back up. He'd cry and try to run to his mother, but his mother would turn him right back around to his father, his real father.

David throws his hands up, ducks his head behind them and keeps his eyes on KG. He dances around like he knows what he's doing. KG throws a punch and it hits his jaw, but David keeps his hands up. He doesn't cry. He doesn't flinch. He just studies the moves of KG. David moves in and punches KG. It lands. It lands right on his shoulder, but it lands. They exchange punch after punch. David lands some, then KG. KG's punches get harder, they inflict pain into David. It doesn't matter, though. It starts to feel good to David. It feels good to be able to take hit after hit.

Before long, they are both looking into each other's eyes and studying each other, anticipating the next move. David is learning.

He is learning from his big brother how to *man up* and not fear anyone.

Thomas gets to the steps and knocks on the door. He is furious, but he has a blank expression on his face.

Tara answers the door. She recognizes the look, she recognizes his demeanor, and steps back.

Thomas grabs her by the neck, lifts her six inches off of the ground and carries her to the nearest wall.

He squeezes tight.

"Who the fuck was that?" he yells. He throws her to the ground.

Struggling to catch her breath, she lifts up slowly.

"It was…"

Thomas punches her back to the ground with so much force that it instantly knocks her out.

He looks at her limp body and starts smacking her.

"Wake up, bitch. Wake up." He smacks her until she wakes up.

As soon as she starts mumbling, he punches her again. This time she doesn't go out. She is totally conscious. He takes her by her arm and drags her to the living room.

He sees that she is coughing up blood and trying to wipe the blood from her brow, but her movements just make him angrier.

"I'm going to ask you one last time. Who the fuck was that?"

All of the lies and excuses that once harbored her mind had been erased. She can't think. "It was the principal. At David's school," she gasps.

"Bitch, you lying. Why would you be riding in the principal's car?"

He punches her again, leaving her bloody and almost unconscious.

He walks into the kitchen.

Tara is fearing the worse. She can hear his daunting footsteps. She can hear the drawers in the kitchen opening. She knows that he is going to kill her.

She tries to move her legs, but they won't budge. She tries to grab the legs of the table, but doesn't have enough strength to pull herself up.

"Aight David, I'm taking you home. When we get there, I'mma talk to your mom about letting you come over on the weekends. You need to get up from under her. Aight?"

David nods his head. He is in pain. His whole body is sore. But he doesn't care. Now he knows who his father was. He knows how strong he was and it only took for him to get beat down by KG.

"David, I'm your big brother. And I'm not gonna let anything happen to you," KG says with a smile.

They pull up into David's driveway and get out of the car. David is first to get to his front door. He pushes the door that is already slightly open. He walks in. Right there in front of him, lying on the wooden floor is his mother with a bloody face and body.

"Mom!" David yells, running to her side.

Thomas sees David and yells, "Get the—"

Then he sees KG. Already, KG has his gun out and pointed at Thomas's chest.

Thomas drops the knife and puts his hands up like he's a criminal who has just gotten busted.

"Don't throw your hands up now." KG puts his gun down. He walks over to Thomas and looks up at the tall, muscular man.

David is watching. He is afraid for KG. And then like an instant flash of lightening, KG punches Thomas in the face.

David's eyes buck like a deer in front of headlights. He watches Thomas stumble back, he sees KG giving him blow after blow to the face. He is surprised to see Thomas do nothing, just covering himself up.

David is in awe. He can't believe Thomas is not punching back. He can't believe that blood is gushing out of the cuts in his face and Thomas is yelling in pain.

After whaling on Thomas, KG takes off his brass knuckles.

"Come here, li'l D. You see this sucka right here?"

Thomas is lying on the ground fluttering around like a fish out of water.

"I want you to punch him."

Without hesitation, David punches him. His fist brings back with it blood and tissue from Thomas's head.

"Keep punching him."

David punches him in the same spot every time. The punches hurt David's fist more than Thomas's head, but each punch makes David feel more like a man.

KG pulls his gun back out. He hands it to David.

"Hit him with it. Like you are swinging a bat. One good time."

David swings the butt of the gun and lands it right in his ear.

Thomas hears a sharp piercing sound and he screams. The sound is disappears.

He continues to scream in agony.

"Damn, David, now how the hell is he going to hear me?" KG says.

KG moves over to Thomas's good ear.

He whispers. "I hope you hear me. I hope you hear me loud and clear. Lay a fucking hand on either one of them again, and I am going to kill you. Myself, me. KG. I'mma kill you."

KG gets up and carries Tara into his car. David follows. It would be the last time Thomas lays a finger on either one of them.

After Christmas break, David finally goes back to school, and Tara goes back to her man.

And David's first day of school is more interesting than it has ever been before.

CHAPTER EIGHTEEN

The first period bell rings, and as usual, the students are slamming lockers, and bumping into each other to make it to class on time. Everyone except David. David takes his time through the hallway, scanning every corner and class. He's walking like he has grown two large balls over Christmas break. He's focused, confident and ready.

"Hey, David," a girl in the hallway says, smiling at him, while standing in the entrance of his Algebra class. "What's up?"

David nods his head and slides right past her. He sits in the back row and stares at the chalkboard. He imagines punching the biggest bully in the school in the face and walking away with his shoes, with his pride.

"Psst. David," another girl whispers to him to get his attention.

David doesn't even look over to the beautiful cheerleader. He does, however, smile inside.

While sitting at the lunchroom table, waiting for Dashawn to appear, David watches Sam grab a tray from the line and head over to a table. She is wearing a bright pink polo shirt with a pair of jeans. Immediately, David's heart beats faster. He misses her, especially since over the summer they barely saw each other or even talked.

"What's up, Sam?" David asks.

"Nothing. I'm trying to hurry up and eat so that I can go to the library."

"You always got your nose in some damn book," David says, forming a smile.

Sam rolls her eyes. "And. Your point is?"

David shakes his head and shuffles in his chair. His intentions were to come to the cafeteria ready for war, but once he met eyes with Sam, something else took over, something that he could not control. His body relaxed; he felt warm inside.

"Aight then. I'mma leave you alone," David says, pulling up from the table.

"No. Stay," Sam says, reaching out for his hand.

David swallows deeply. This is the very first time Sam has ever looked at him twice, especially like that. The butterflies in his stomach start fluttering. He stays.

As Sam takes a couple of bites out of her ham and cheese sandwich, David's nerves are keeping him from realizing his hunger. He doesn't care. Just being with her makes him happy. The way she pauses to look at him and laughs at the jokes he doesn't even think are funny, he can tell that she is finally feeling him. Everything is funny. Everything is calm. Until David turns his head toward a tall shadow that is walking up to the table.

"I hear you looking for me," Dashawn says with a deep voice, showing more muscles than David had remembered.

David looks up at him. But before David can get up, he hears a chair pull back and feels the table move. Like jack in the box, Sam pops up out of nowhere and is in Dashawn's face.

"Dashawn, ain't nobody scared of you," Sam yells, pointing her finger in his face.

"Girl, sit down," Dashawn says.

David gently grabs Sam's hand. She snatches it away.

"No, I'm not about to let him just disrespect you like that."

David calmly grabs her hand again.

"I got this. Chill out."

David says it so calmly that one would think he was soothing a baby.

"You ain't got shit," Dashawn says, laughing with his friends. "You looking for me. Here I am," Dashawn beats his chest twice with his fist.

David looks down at the shoes that are on Dashawn's feet.

"I want my shoes back," David says.

The shoes don't look as new and clean. Rather, they look like they have molded to Dashawn's feet.

David and Dashawn are now surrounded by everyone in the cafeteria. The students are waiting. They are waiting on someone, anyone to swing. Forget the talking. They want to see a fight.

"Take 'em," Dashawn blurts out.

"Break it up. Break it up. There won't be a fight today," Mr. Harrington says, plowing through the amped up crowd.

"David. I need to speak with you in my office."

He looks at Dashawn, finally putting two and two together.

"Matter of fact, I need to talk to the both of you."

As they walk down the hall, the principal tries talking to them. "Now, what's the problem between you two?"

David looks at Dashawn with the coldest stare. Such a stare that Dashawn is actually getting a little nervous. He is boggled by the sudden boldness of David.

"So, neither of you want to talk, huh? We're going to play that game?"

Once they get to the office, neither boy mentions anything about the shoes, so Mr. Harrington gives up.

"Dashawn, go to your class. David, you stay with me."

Mr. Harrington waits for Dashawn to leave, then quietly shuts the door.

"How's your mother doing?"

"She cool," David says, looking like he is being interrogated for a crime but is refusing to give up anything.

He just stares and waits for the next question, emotionless and hard.

"What about your father?"

"My father is dead."

Mr. Harrington yanks his head back. The David he talked to before Christmas break is a totally different David than is sitting before him now.

"Well, tell your mother to call me." Mr. Harrington hands David a card with the school information on it and takes in a deep breath. "Okay, I guess you can go back to class."

School has let out and David stands by the door of the gym.

He tries to be discreet, but the beautiful girls who keep waving at him are distracting.

Suddenly, he is becoming the talk of the school, and the eyes that he once craved are now on him. Even the boys are speaking to him. "This is how KG must feel," David says, waiting beside a bush.

The more attention David gets, the more he becomes confident in the fact that he is his father's child.

Finally, Dashawn shows up. As usual, he is surrounded by his male groupies.

Not wanting to get jumped, David decides to call him out.

"Eh, Da-shawn!"

Dashawn darts towards him, expecting that his fast speed and hard stare will scare him, force David to back down. It doesn't.

David walks right up to him and as soon as he gets close enough, David two pieces him. *Bop. Bop.* He is extremely accurate in hitting him in the nose. Everyone can tell by the blood gushing out of his meaty looking gash.

Dashawn finds his nose to make sure it is still there. The hit surprises him. No one has ever hit him back. He isn't used to the pain. He looks at David, who is bouncing around, fully focusing on him.

David doesn't see anyone besides him and Dashawn. Not even Sam, who is yelling his name. All he sees is the next punch drilling into Dashawn's head.

The instigating yells get to Dashawn, so he throws up his bloody hands. But as soon as Dashawn's fists reach the corners of his chin, David lunges in at him and punches him square in the face.

Dashawn's feet become wobbly as they try to find a secure stance and everyone is yelling for David and chanting for Dashawn to fight back. But he can't.

Again, David dances around Dashawn, waiting for an opening. Dashawn's weak hands drop slightly. David steps in so fast Dashawn can't react. With his right fist, David punches Dashawn in the jaw, sending him flying to the ground.

Dashawn tries to get back up, tries to look around for help, but David jumps on him, straddles him, and punches with such great force that Dashawn's lip is splitting and the areas around his eyes are growing purple.

Now Dashawn is yelling. He is screaming for help. His nose has shifted and the pain is so excruciating that his numb face can't feel the tears that are streaming down.

It takes two security guards and Mr. Harrington to get David off of the bloody boy.

"My shoes, I ain't leaving without my shoes."

David starts yelling, kicking, and fighting to be let free.

The guard can't hear David through all of the commotion and all of the "oohing" and yelling from the pumped up crowd.

"Now that's what I'm talking about," some of the kids screamed. "D-a-y-u-m!" others yell, laughing and talking boisterously amongst each other.

Dashawn stays on the ground, holding his nose. Blood runs from his nose to his hands, arms, and elbows.

"I want my shoes," David says, watching Dashawn bury his face into someone's t-shirt.

"Damn, I knew it," Mr. Harrington says.

Again, Mr. Harrington walks the two boys to his office and yells for the secretary to call the ambulance.

"What's the matter with you two?" Mr. Harrington says slamming his fist onto his desk.

This time David speaks up.

"Man, all I know is that you better take my shoes off. I want my shoes." David is fuming, red in the face and punching his knuckles in the inside of his other hand.

The nurse comes flying into the office with rolls of bandages and fresh towels.

David looks at Dashawn again. He yells, "I want my mothafuckin' shoes."

"Hold up. You not just going to be in my office cur—" Mr. Harrington stops in the middle of his sentence. He has to. What he is witnessing, especially after the last principal briefed him on Dashawn, he needs a second to digest it.

Dashawn uses his free hand and one by one he takes his shoes off.

"So that's what this whole thing is about," Mr. Harrington says. He is speechless. He is witnessing the biggest bully in the school give in to David.

David gets up and takes his shoes. Then he takes one of the towels from the chair that the nurse left for Dashawn's nose and wipes them down like he is polishing a trophy.

"Now that's definitely Greg's son," Mr. Harrington mumbles.

Mr. Harrington can't wait to call Tara.

"Hello. May I speak with Mrs. Peterson?"

"This is she!"

Mr. Harrington doesn't recognize her cheerful voice. He hesitates.

"This is Mr. Harrington. David has gotten into a serious fight. I need you to come pick him up from my office."

Tara raises her voice, "David? Okay, I'm on my way."

Mr. Harrington remembers that she doesn't own a car.

"You know what? I'll bring him home."

"That will work, too," Tara says.

An hour later, Mr. Harrington takes David home as promised.

The three sit down and listen as Mr. Harrington replays the incident like it was a famous boxing match.

"I was wondering what happened to those shoes," Tara says. She looks at David and shakes her head.

Tara then signals for David to go to his room.

As soon as David is in his room, Mr. Harrington whispers. "Tara, I have been trying to contact you. Is everything all right?"

Tara smiles. "Everything is perfect. I kicked Thomas out. I'm planning on starting school in the summer and—" She pauses.

"Well, I thought David was doing fine."

Mr. Harrington looks at her and gives her a smirk. "He is doing very well. He reminded me of Greg today in high school. I am proud of him. You have no idea."

Tara gives Mr. Harrington a big hug. A little too big for David, who is watching from the hallway.

Before leaving, he reiterates, "If you need anything, call me."

Tara assures him that she will. Mr. Harrington yells to the back to David. He says goodbye and then walks out the door. He is happy that he doesn't have to kill Thomas and happy that he can keep his job.

David and Dashawn are suspended for three days, but once they return, David is the popular one. People are still afraid of Dashawn, but when both names come up in conversation, David is definitely *that dude*.

On the first day coming back to school, David doesn't boast. He doesn't even mention the fight. He just wears his shoes with style. He doesn't have to say anything. No one messes with him anymore or talks bad about him.

And as far as the girls, he has a nice set of groupies. But again, his heart is dead set on Sam. She is all he wants. She is all he ever wanted. But getting her is a whole 'nother story.

CHAPTER NINETEEN

High School

"Have you ever wondered what it would be like to be one of Donald Trump's kids? Or Puff Daddy's? Just some rich kid that don't have to worry about nothing. Not a damn thing? They go to jail for the stupidest shit and don't even have to do time," Sam says.

David stares at the wall into space, and then glances back at Sam. "Now what were you saying?"

"David! It's like we literally start from the bottom. We never have enough, but we are expected to go out here, suck it up, and become this great person."

David raises his eyebrow. He shrugs his shoulder, "Aight. Be that great person."

Sam smacks her lips. "So what you trying to tell me is that people from the hood have the same opportunities as people born with rich parents that live in nice neighborhoods?"

David looks up at the ceiling to think about it. "What I'm saying is that yeah, we starting from the bottom. But, there are so many people that are born at the top and can't handle it. Their lives were too damn easy. They didn't have to struggle. The way I see it is we were born in this shit. So if we make it out, that means we had to be strong. So we can handle the things that rich kids can't handle." He smiles. "Plus, we have more fun when we make it. We appreciate what we got."

Sam nods her head. Then smiles. "Wow, David. I didn't think you had it in you." She studies David's silly smirk, then smacks her lips. "You got that from Cathy."

David tries to hold his serious stare, but then cracks a smile.

Sam continues to talk about her life and her struggle and David just sits there and listens. He admires her big dreams, her determination. He thinks it's sexy.

"You're a different kind of chick, Sam," David interrupts.

Sam's face lights up.

"A weird kinda chick," David says, cracking up at the same time.

From her window Sam can see the tall buildings that make up East Mount Projects. She tries to bite her tongue, but the thoughts in her mind are too much to just let go.

"David, I get so damn tired of coming up in here with no electricity," she says, sitting up over him as he lay on her bed. "Can't use the microwave, can't cook and some nights I have to sleep in the kitchen with the oven wide open so that I don't freeze to death. And don't let me forget where I put the candles and the lighter before the sun goes down. I be searching for days in the dark."

David's smile turns into a serious gaze. Her words make him feel helpless.

"And how the hell am I supposed to do my homework?" she says. "By the time I come home from work, it's so dark in here, I start seeing and hearing shit. The floors be talking to me, the walls start caving in, and shit just starts appearing out of nowhere."

Sam pauses to laugh at her own situation. She looks into David's eyes. He is tuning into her every word. "Sometimes I look at Courtney and she just pisses me off. Why can't she just get herself together?" Sam sighs while pulling on a loose thread on her blanket. "I don't know. I just know that if I keep studying I can get that scholarship to go to Ohio State and I can be gone forever, never come back. Never have to worry about depending on nobody."

"Damn, Sam, you on your period?" David blurts out.

"Nah, bruh," she says, punching him in the chest.

They both let out a laugh.

"You need to pull out your mother's journal and start reading it, sumthin'. Maybe it will calm your little ass down," David says.

"I've read it. I've read it so much, I know it by heart. I've been looking everywhere for the other journals, but can't find them. I think Courtney hid them." She rubs her fingers against her chin. "There is just one place I haven't..."

"David, are we going to get to your homework or what? You know you can't miss another assignment in Mr. Griggs class, he ain't playin' whichu."

David sits up in the bed and instantly seems to be in a hurry.

"I gotta go. I gotta make some runs before I have to help my moms. She probably at home now." He walks to the door. "I'll call you, though."

The bulging copper padlock catches his eye. He turns around, "Your momma still have you lock yourself in your room?"

Sam shakes her head. "Nah, I do it just out of habit."

Frustrated with Sam's situation, David heads out the door. *Man, if only I could hustle up enough money. She'd be out of this damn house.* On his way down the steps, he slides a tiny clear bag up under Courtney's door. He looks behind him to make sure Sam is still in her room. He then runs down the second flight of steps and through the kitchen. On his tippy toes, he reaches over the stove and the greasy hood and pulls out a medicine bottle. It is hidden behind a stack of Pork n Beans and a tall bottle of soy sauce.

He uses his index finger to pull the bills out, counts them to make sure it is all there, and then heads out the door. Shutting the front door behind him and looking around to make sure no one is watching him or plotting on him, he jumps off the porch and gets in his black Camry with windows so dark, it's barely legal. He grabs the remote to his Pioneer stereo, presses the play button, and immediately it starts banging Goodie Mob. He leans back, pops a blunt in his mouth, and moves his head to the rhythm. The bass starts bumping. The streets start vibrating. From upstairs, Sam can hear him as he pulls off and can still hear him as he whips around the corner.

"Hey, son, I hear you coming all the way down the street. Where were you at, Sam's house?" Tara asks.

"Yep, you know she tryna help me pass English."

"I know." Tara shakes her head. "Sam seems like the best person to help you - and she's pretty too."

David mumbles, "I know."

"What are you cooking?" Tara asks. "That chili from yesterday was out of this world. It had a little kick to it, but it was good. Who taught you how to cook like that?"

"You, Ma." David smiles.

David watches his mother pull out her big clunky books and spread them across the kitchen table. She slides on her eye glasses and with pen and paper in hand starts flipping the pages and jotting down notes. He turns back around and turns on the stove. He then starts daydreaming about his mother's past.

"Come on, David, we have to catch this bus. I will not go another day without getting this done," Tara said, rushing out of the house.

"Where are we going?" David asked.

"We are going to the police station."

David could barely keep up with her long strides and hear her through her quick breaths.

"I'll tell you when we get on the bus."

Just as the bus closed its squeaky doors, Tara tapped on the glass. She found a seat for her and her young son and then began to talk.

"Now listen here."

Tara looked into her son's dark brown eyes.

"David. If I ever see or hear you put your hands on a woman, I just might kill you myself. I mean it. A man never has the right to hit on a woman. I don't care what that woman does. You better learn to walk away."

Tara tilted her head up for a second to take in fresh air.

"For years I had to deal with a man that hit me, that talked down on me and I allowed it. I let him."

"Why didn't you leave?" David asked, relieved to finally be able to ask the question that had been lingering in his mind since he could remember.

Tara paused to think about it. "I loved him. He was so different when I first met him. He loved me. So when he would hit me, I knew that deep down, he still loved me. I thought that if I did this, or did that, he would change, but the more I gave, the more he took, and the more he took, the weaker I became."

Tara was almost in tears. Although people were coming on and off the bus, and the bus was waving from side to side at times from the bumps and constant changes in weight, Tara and David were in another world. Tara truly took advantage of the connection she had with her son and tried her best to get him to understand how passionate she was about their past.

"Never, ever let someone imprison you like that."

David didn't know what "imprison" meant, but he didn't want to interrupt her either.

"If a person loves you, they will show you. You won't have to guess. It's not freaking rocket science. It is what it is. What you see is what you get. But it's up to you to see. It's up to you to be smart enough, aware enough to read between the lines. Finding love is great, but don't make the mistake, the same mistake that I constantly make, of making it the priority. Your priority in life is finding who you are and first loving yourself. Sometimes you can be so thirsty for love that you misconstrue pure common sense."

Tara let out a chuckle.

"It's just such a shame that it took one too many beatings for me to realize it. And that's why we are getting a restraining order."

David dips the pork chops into the battered eggs in a deep white bowl and then throws them into a bag of flour. He shakes the bag back and forth in the air and then one by one drops the pork chops in the grease.

Still thinking about his mother, he watches the grease gather around the flour and fry it to a crisp. He stares at it as it bleeds and then hardens. His mind drifts off into his past yet again. Once again, he relives what happened years ago.

"No, Thomas. You are not coming over here. I will send you your things. Stop calling here," Tara said.

The strength of her voice was weak, but the more he called, the easier it was for her to say no. She had finally found power in that word.

Many nights David heard her crying. He didn't know what to do, though. So he did what his mother and Thomas did for him when he was crying or was hurt. Nothing.

The time came when Thomas stopped calling and coming around. It seemed like he had finally given up. But it's never that easy.

"You can pick me up. I'll be ready at seven o'clock."

David listened to Tara's words while slapping some peanut butter onto a piece of bread, smashing the jellied slice onto it, and then slowly pushing it into his mouth. Each chew was deliberately controlled. He didn't want the sound of his jaw to get in the way of his hearing.

"What should I wear? Oh. Okay." Tara hung up the phone.

David watched his mother move from side to side with excitement.

He was worried. *Who the hell is taking my mother out?* The question was burning inside, but he kept it under control. Even though he was hardly scared of his mother, he always respected her.

At exactly six forty-five, Tara stepped out of her room. A cloud of sweet body wash and flowery perfume followed her. She looked good. With her slim waistline and her voluptuous curves, Tara walked around the dining room, glowing. The many days she spent at the gym to let out the stress the breakup caused had really done her body some good. David could do nothing but smile.

Shortly after, the bell rang.

"Get the door, David!" Tara yelled from the back.

David opened the door slowly.

"Mr. Harrington?"

"What's up, David," his principal said, dressed in a suit and tie.

David began to crack a smile. Then he remembered his new found position in the house. Hardening his face, standing up tall, to make up for lost inches, and deepening his voice, David opened his mouth and said, "What do you want?"

"I would like to take your mother out. Would that be all right with you?"

David slightly closed the door and looked back at his mother. She was standing tall with her dark red stilettos on and her dress that was hugging every inch of her body.

David turned back around, trying to keep away the smile.

"Yes, sir. You may."

Tara walked gracefully to the door and Mr. Harrington took her hand.

It was the first time David had seen a man treat her mother like she was valuable. As he watched the two walk away holding hands, he thought to himself, *I wonder if my father treated her that good.*

David watched the Lexus roll away and then he plopped down on the couch. He turned on the television, but then jumped up when he heard a knock at the door. Without thinking, he swung the door open, assuming it was his mother. But it wasn't. A wobbly, unstable man stood there, waving a paper bag with the head of a glass bottle hanging out the top.

"What do you want?" David said.

"I want your motha—"

Thomas struggled to stand on his feet.

"I need her."

David looked at the man he once called father. Gray hair had replaced the dark strong strands he remembered, wrinkles had formed, and his clothes smelled of liquor and musty armpits.

David's expression softened. His words were gentle.

"I'mma need you to leave."

As David turned around, he caught a glimpse of a shining object. It was a gun. Just that fast, Thomas pulled a 9mm straight from under his shirt.

The gun was pointed directly at David's forehead. It was cold and hard against his skin. At first David was shook, but then once he saw that Thomas was unstable, he quickly snatched the gun, pushed Thomas down the steps and watched as his hands flew up in the air.

"Don't shoot. Please!" Thomas pleaded.

David shook his head at his pitiful looking stepfather. He allowed him to get up and walk away. David stood there on the porch, standing tall like the man of his house, and watched as Thomas wobbled down the street.

At that point, David knew that liquor was not the only thing running through Thomas's veins.

David looked at the gun, examining its curves and the trigger.

The weight of the gun made him feel powerful. Made him feel like a man. Made his worries that maybe Thomas would come back be stomped out by the fact that if he came back and try some slick shit with his mother, he'd shoot him dead. That was the last time David saw Thomas, and the last time Tara went on a date.

"I have to get myself together first," she told David when asked about dating again.

David finishes frying up the pork chops and spoons the cheesy macaroni and cheese into his mouth.

"Dinner is almost ready, Mom," David says proudly.

"Boy, do I love me some you," Tara says.

David walks over to her, hugs her from the back, and gives her a kiss on the cheek.

"I love you too, Ma." He looks at her sagging eyes from working the night shift and from attending school during the day. "Mom, one day you won't have to work anymore. I promise."

Tara pats him on his hand. "Your momma is a big girl. I can handle it." She puts on a weak smile from her weariness and then gets back to work.

David finishes up the kitchen, wiping down the table, catching all corners and then places the damp rag underneath the sink.

While kneeling down, he hears something move. It is coming from outside.

Ever since David started selling drugs, he has become paranoid. Being the man of the house came with great responsibilities, so he grabs his 9mm and walks boldly out of the house.

David hears someone whisper, "Big D." The person is in his bushes.

He doesn't even have to turn around. He knows who it is.

"Damn," David says, spinning back around while sucking air through his teeth.

He looks at the woman's droopy eyes and she looks into his. She keeps hitting herself, fidgeting and scratching the same spot on her head.

"What do you want?" David asks.

"Come on, D," she says.

"What?" he says, looking at the bones that are poking out from her skin. "Sheri, you need to be *gone*. You can't be out here like that. I keep telling your ass. Not at my mom's house."

"You don't have any? Not even a little?" she stutters.

David turns around and goes back into the house.

Through his window, he watches her stumble through the bed of flowers, and through her old yard. She gets so close to the living room window, almost kissing it, and cups her hands against it so that she can focus in on what is going on inside. Her hair is all over the place, jeans falling off of her tiny waist, and her shoes are worn down to the bare sole. She reminds David of the outdoor furniture that once looked new, but then becomes damaged by the unpredictable weather.

All of a sudden a car pulls up. It's Daniel. He pulls up in a brand new Mercedes.

Before he can park the car, his mother runs up to his window.

"Ma, what you doing here?" Daniel says.

"Give me a couple of dollars," she says.

He pulls out a wad of cash, hands a couple of bills to her, just so he wouldn't have to bear being around her.

Satisfied, she tries kissing him, but he rolls up the window. As he is pulling into the garage, Sheri trots back to David's screen.

"Naw, I'm cool," he says to her, pointing to the end of the street.

Daniel watches his mother finally leave and walks past David's door. They see each other, but don't acknowledge one another.

Daniel knows that Sheri is one of David's customers and he hates him for it. David doesn't care. He hates Daniel just on the strength that he thinks he is better than everyone else, especially poor people.

The day that Daniel's grandfather got killed by a group of thugs, David saw him morph into a hot headed, "I'm better than everyone else," kind of dude. Flaunting his money from his grandfather's will, and now attending one of the best private schools in the state, he has no respect for anyone, including his father. David and Daniel's hate for each other runs deep

CHAPTER TWENTY

Eleventh grade.

The last period bell rings and the school hallway floods with anxious students. Everyone has one purpose in mind, to hurry up and get off of school property. Sam is no different. Dressed casual with just a light purple, fitting sweater and khakis, she too is carrying her books snug to her chest and swiftly walking down the school walkway.

She cups her hand to block the blinding sunlight. Then she notices a hand waving in the air for her. She squints and lifts her hand up a little more. Once she sees that it's David, she sighs. "Ugh." She rolls her eyes to the sky. "He gets on my nerves."

Leaning against the hood of his car, David is surrounded by the most popular and giddiest girls at school. He is wearing a white t-shirt, a slim gold chain that's glistening in the sun, and a pair of jeans that's doing a poor job of covering his butt. Instead, it's exposing his powder blue cotton boxers. His muscles are bulging out of his sleeves while his six pack is forming ripples through his shirt.

Shaking her head and laughing to herself, Sam walks past the girls, keeping an eye on them. She mumbles, "That dude sho know how to pick 'em."

"Aight ladies," David tells the groupies who are reluctant to move for Sam. "I'll holla at ya lata." The group of girls walks away. But before leaving, the newest girl in school gives Sam an evil stare. She sees Sam and immediately mumbles, "Why would he want a nerdy girl like her? I bet she still a virgin." She puts her hand on her hips, while still staring at Sam. "You gon' have to just move me."

Sam instantly returns the look. But with more intensity. "You don't know me like that," Sam says, daring the girl to say something.

The girl looks back, surprised at Sam's response. Not being familiar with Sam, the girl rolls her eyes and turns away, catching up with the rest of the crowd.

"You so gangsta, I love it," David says laughing.

"What do you want?" Sam snaps.

David's smile instantly fades. He gets up from the hood of the car and gently grabs Sam's hand. She yanks back from him and starts walking off.

"I don't have time for you, your groupies, or the fact that you couldn't care less about school. Why am I wasting my time trying to help you pass math and you don't even care?"

Sam walks away, frustrated with him, yet wanting him to fight for her. She loves him, but she loves her dream more. All David can see is her back, her long black silky hair swaying through the wind as she walks.

"I passed!" David shouts loudly like he's yelling to heaven.

Sam stops and twists back around.

Her expression is priceless to David. Her smile always finds a way to warm his heart. He looks at her, admiring her beauty as she smiles at him. She still reminds him of Pocahontas.

"You passed!"

"Yep, thanks to you. I got a seventy-six. I'll be a senior next year. Holla-at-cha-boi!"

Sam's smile grows. Then she freezes. She isn't sure what she should do next. Finally, the awkwardness between the two eases. She drops her books on to the grass and throws her arms around him.

"I am so proud of you. I knew you were smart! Hard-headed, but smart."

David grabs her waist, holds her tight, and rests his head on her quite differently than she had expected. She pulls back.

Feeling rather uncomfortable, Sam turns around and walks away again. Once again, David finds himself chasing her.

"Why do you give me such a hard time, Sam? What's up with you?"

Sam crosses the street, making sure not to move too fast. David crosses, too.

"Sam!" he shouts.

After making it to the sidewalk, she turns to him. She looks him straight in the face, like a mother would a child she is disappointed with.

"What?" she says with an attitude.

"Sam, everyone in the school knows I like you, that I want to be with you, but you."

Sam looks at him as if he is a joke. "I can't tell. You always having hoes around, kissing the ground you walk on."

David laughs, catches himself, and then gets serious again.

"You got it right, they're hoes. I know who they are and you know who they are. That's all they are to me, hoes. But you. I want you to be my girl. They can be gone tomorrow, too easy."

Sam rolls her eyes to him again. "David, you on some other stuff. I really don't have time for a boyfriend, especially a hustler."

She scans the neighborhood. Then she steps up close to him and looks so deeply into his eyes as if talking to his soul. Her voice projects through the neighborhood as she proclaims to the world how she feels.

"Look at where we at. Do you see it? Do you notice the thirsty dudes robbing for a couple-a-dollas, the murders, the crackheads down the hill, the little kids that don't really have a future? Or are you so lost in your own little world that you can't see this neighborhood falling apart?"

Sam turns her attention to the now deteriorating neighborhood.

"This ain't the type of life I want, not for me and not for my kids. And you. You're part of the problem. You don't care. You know you're my best friend and all, but the way you live, the way you think, you gon' always be stuck in some shit. I can't be with someone that ain't trying to go nowhere in life. You out here selling drugs to people that have to go home and be mothers to their kids; you out here slanging dope just to buy shoes, jewelry, get girls. I mean hoes. And for what?"

She pauses, but doesn't get an answer. Even more frustrated, she starts waving her hands again.

"Where you gon' be at in five years? Didn't think about that, did you? Well, did you think about where the child of that crackhead you sold drugs to gon' be in five years? Did you think about who that child is going to grow up and become, who he gonna kill because his mother was strung out and he feels alone and neglected? Where's your mind at? Where's your goals? Who are you? If you don't know, then what the hell do you think you can offer me?"

David's expression is blank. He is at a loss for words.

Feeling embarrassed, he just stands there. He is frustrated. He hears Sam, but he just can't understand where she is coming from. This is his home and he can't really see how bad it is. He thought he had moved up once he moved to the suburbs and even though it is the borderline, it still seems good enough. At least for now.

Sam turns around and walks away.

David lets her. He no longer wants to stop her.

Damn, that's the person she sees when she looks at me. Damn, that's fucked up. He watches Sam walk away.

It takes him a minute, but after walking back to his car, he is finally able to see himself through her eyes. He begins to see his neighborhood differently. He begins to see his future.

A week later at school, David is still nowhere to be found. Sam feels bad. *Maybe I laid it on him a li'l too thick.* She watches the crowds of kids rushing into the lunch room, wishing that David would just appear. *I messed up. My mouth always getting me in trouble,* she thinks while dipping her spoon in and out of the pool of chocolate pudding. *I miss him. He hasn't called in a week, came over, nothing. I hope he's all right.* Sam starts to think about his smile, his jokes and even the occasional hugs. She shakes her head and closes her eyes. *Yeah. I messed up.*

"Ladies and gentlemen, can I have your attention please?"

Everyone including Sam follows the voice to the entrance of the cafeteria. It instantly becomes quiet. Other than a couple of snickers and whispers sprinkling around, everyone is silent, waiting for something big to happen.

All of a sudden, a huge smile covers Sam's face. It is David. Dressed in a black and white suit and tie, clean as ever. He makes a signal to a boy also dressed in a suit.

Sam is in awe. She is slightly embarrassed, but watches four muscular and handsome boys from the football team walk toward her, wearing the same outfit, and each bearing a gift.

One by one they approach her like a queen on a throne and hand her a gift. At the same time, David, who now has a mic in his hand, starts talking, explaining to Sam and everyone in the cafeteria what each item represents.

"The seven roses represents each year you have been my best friend. The six chocolate candies are for your sweet lips I want to kiss."

Everyone starts laughing. He continues until finally he is at number one.

Sam's eyes are pouring with tears. The whole cafeteria is 'oohing' and 'ahhing.' Every girl witnessing this special moment is wishing it were her.

David kneels down to her and pulls out a black square box. Down on one knee, he says, "Sam, I love you. I don't care about the streets. I only care about you. If anybody can help me get my shit together, I know it would be you."

Sam covers her mouth. She shakes her head and stares back at David.

David eases the box open. Sitting snug in the padded black pillow is a shiny gold ring with a tiny diamond on top. Sam is speechless. This is so unexpected and so out of the ordinary. This is something that she reads in romance books, not something that actually happens. Especially not for a girl whose life always seems to shake with disappointment and tragedy.

"Sam, this ring is a promise to you that as long as you stay the great woman that you are, I will be the man that you deserve. Will you be my girlfriend?" David takes his finger and smoothes the tears from Sam's cheeks.

Sam smiles. She hesitates, studying the sincerity of his voice.

"Yes, David."

David jumps up. "Yes!"

Even though he has gone through great lengths to get Sam, he didn't believe he was capable of snatching up the girl of his dreams. In his mind, she is not just any girl. She is different. She is someone he can see spending the rest of his life with.

David wraps his arms around Sam. He holds her tight. He reaches down and kisses her. Her lips are as sweet as he'd dreamed.

He had kissed plenty of girls before her, but kissing her literally melts his heart, makes his legs weak, but no one in the room is going to see that softer side of him.

For the rest of the day, David does what he normally doesn't do: He goes to each class and he is on time. "Damn, I love that girl. She gon' be the mother of my kids. I'm going to take care of her. She ain't gon' want for shit," he mumbles, daydreaming while the teacher demonstrates an algebraic equation.

After school, David waits for Sam to get out of class. He can't wait to see his girl. He so badly wants to kiss her again, but she has such an intimidating personality, even he becomes afraid at times to touch her in that way.

Sam finally comes out of the school doors glowing brighter than a full moon on a dark lonely night.

The closer she gets to David, the faster his heart beats. Inside he feels like a boy that has just won over the heart of a princess, but from the outside, he is just smiling. *I can't be looking too soft out here.*

Sam gets to the car. There are no jealous girls lurking around him, begging for a ride or trying to get David for an after school special. Instead, it is just the two love birds, suddenly acting shy and quiet. David opens the door for his queen and Sam takes it all in.

Sam has always loved David, but was too focused to allow the thoughts of being with him to really stir her emotions. But how can she not be with him now? He is changing. He is attempting to get himself together. And she makes sure of it. As she smiles at her prince, she wastes no time in laying down the law.

"If you are going to be with me, you have to quit hustling. I can't be with you if you out here in the streets."

David knew it was coming. He looks at her, wanting to mute her sound and just look at her pretty face. *She is messing up the whole vibe.*

David shakes his head. "All right, but I have to first get rid of what I got."

Sam can tell by the way David's voice changed that she is killing the mood. She looks out of the window. "All right."

Months later, David and Sam are still the most envied couple at school.

They are that couple that kisses in the hallways, that holds hands to class, and that goes to every school event together - sometimes wearing matching colors. And David does as promised; he treats her like a queen. He wears more button downs than hoodies, and on occasion sports a tie. He really has stepped up his game.

He does, however, miss the mark when it comes to his occupation of choice. He had told her that he wasn't going to sell any drugs anymore after he got rid of all of the drugs he had. However, he didn't tell her that he had a good six months left on the job. He didn't see anything wrong with it, though, because it would allow him to take care of her like he had always dreamed.

Chapter Twenty One

"**C**lose your eyes, babe," David says after Sam gets into the car.

A bright smile instantly forms on Sam's face. "Where are we going? You're scaring me," Sam says, brushing her hands against the seat.

"Don't worry about it. I'm going to take good care of you," David says.

"You sound like a psycho." In a deep distorted voice Sam repeats, "I am going to take good care of you."

They both laugh.

While in the car, David tells Sam jokes to keep her laughing, they reminisce about the many months they have spent together going to the movies, skating and the late night walks at the lake.

"Remember the family reunion we went to with Cathy and KG?" Sam asks, eyes still hidden under a folded cloth. "That cook-out was off the chain. I ain't never ate so much in my damn life. Everywhere I turned someone was saying, 'Here take home some food.' Now that's what I call a family."

There is a sudden pause in the car as Sam takes a deep breath. KG and Cathy's family reunion reminds her of what she doesn't have, but wanted so badly: a family.

After thirty minutes of talking and laughing, they finally get to their destination. David gets out first, wraps his arm around her, and then slowly guides her up the steps and into a walkway.

"You can open your eyes now," David whispers into her ear.

Sam opens them. Her eyes widen. She is taken back. She doesn't say a word.

"Well, do you like it?" David asks, anxiously waiting for her to jump up and down and give him a kiss.

"Um. What is this?" Sam says.

"It's a *condo.*"

"I know what it is," she says finally walking forward. "Why are we here?"

The look on Sam's face is straight disappointment. Not the reaction David is expecting. He had really planned for this. He even hired the most expensive maid service and bought their platinum package to spice it up a little.

In the kitchen on the deeply engraved dining room table is an elegant vase that only an interior decorator would choose. It has a dozen roses blooming from it. The room is filled with a soft lavender scent that hit both of their noses as soon as they walked through the door and to even his surprise, there are rose pedals leading to the bedroom. The brand new bedspread that he bought is perfectly made like they have just arrived to a 5 star hotel. Placed on it is a silver platter full of chocolate covered strawberries. After looking at their warm feeling apartment, David is sure that Sam is happy. Then he looks at her. Her face is still twisted.

"Let's look around first," David says, knowing that after seeing the luxurious apartment, she would change her attitude.

Sam agrees.

David walks her to the large kitchen area with a marble island, stainless steel appliances, and over-sized cabinets. Then he walks her to the bedroom with a deep walk-in closet. He throws out his hand. "Now this is a damn closet!"

He even sees her smile once she looks through the huge glass door in her bedroom that allows her the view of the city. David takes advantage of the moment by whispering, "You can wake up in the morning, sit out on the porch, and read a book or something." He glances at Sam again and just shakes his head. *I am so damn tired of trying to make her smile.*

"What's wrong? I thought you would be happy," he says, showing his frustration. "All you ever talk about is getting out of the hood and moving up in the world." He points to the window with the great view. "Well, this is a very good start. I can promise you there ain't no crackheads anywhere near this neighborhood. And if we just so happen to have kids, the school system is one of the best in the city. I checked."

David stands there proud of himself. Just proud that he is barely seventeen and is able to pull something like this off.

Sam rolls her eyes and takes a deep breath.

"But this is not what I wanted," she complains. She slaps her thigh. "I don't want to move in with you and leave my stepmother. I want to move out of the state and go to college. I want to buy a house and be able to do it without using drug money." Sam narrows her eyes to David. "I ain't stupid."

David rubs the top of his head. He can't understand how he tried to do something so good, but it turned out so terribly bad. "So you telling me, you not going to leave that crackhead dungeon of a house to live here? Do you know what girls would do to have a place like this, to have a dude like me?"

Sam cut her eyes at him. She is livid. Her words get choppy and snappy. "Just take me home. Just take me home. Now!"

Sam has had enough. She can't believe the words that have just left his mouth. Crackheads are a touchy subject for her. She lives with one. She witnesses the horrific affects. "How dare he talk to me like that. I ain't just one of his hoes," she rants in the car while waiting for him.

The whole drive back home, Sam just sits there almost in tears. She can't wait to get home to her "crackhead dungeon." She nods her head after staring David down as he drives.

David takes Sam home and is mad as hell, too. *I ain't doing shit else for her*, he promised himself. *Ungrateful ass. The shit I have to go through.* David talked so much shit to himself, he was so adamant about no longer treating her good, but then the next time he would see her beautiful face, he instantly had a change of heart. He loved her. He was in love with her and it was going to take much more than an ungrateful spirit to deter him away from one day marrying the girl.

After a week of not being on good terms and after a long, hard day at school, David drives Sam home. For the whole ride, he is quiet.

"What's up David?" Sam asks.

Still looking straight ahead at the road, David shrugs his shoulders and says, "Nothing. Just got shit on my mind."

Sam's heart starts racing. As she sits there all she can think of is all of the girls who said they wanted him. The girls that intentionally wore the skimpiest clothes they could find just to entice David. "You cheating on me, David?" she blurts out.

David sucks air through his teeth. He looks at her and shakes his head. "Naw, girl." He lets out a small chuckle. "You trippin' for real, Sam."

Once they get into her house, David checks every room to make sure no one is there.

Sam puckers her lips to give David a kiss, but he moves his head. She immediately snaps. "David! What's up with you?"

David smiles. "Oh, my fault. I didn't know you wanted a kiss."

He leans in, gives her a weak kiss, and then leaves.

"I got homework to do. I will call you later," he says, walking back to his car.

Sam let him leave, but watches him through the dingy curtain in the kitchen window. "Something about him is a little off," she says.

In an attempt to focus on an upcoming test, she puts aside her intuition and heads upstairs to do her homework.

An hour into her homework, her stomach growls. She rubs it and then decides to go downstairs to get something to eat. On her way down, she begins to worry. *I hope Courtney didn't eat my chicken sandwich. Payday isn't until Friday.* She shakes her head as she lands on each step. *I knew I should have took that money David tried to give me.* She smacks her lips and shakes her head again.

Sam braces herself while opening up the refrigerator. The cold air oozes out, the light turns on and instantly her eyes grow wide. And so does her smile.

"Food?"

In the refrigerator there is fresh fruit, the greenest vegetables she had ever seen in her refrigerator, and then when she looks in the freezer, there are stacks upon stacks of meat.

All she can do is smile. "David is always up to something," she says, thanking God for such a good boyfriend.

"You crazy," Sam says to David on the phone. "But I love you for it."

"It's cool. I can't be having my lady over there hungry."

Sam turns the oven on and sits the pot on the stove. "Why don't you come over here and I'll make you dinner?"

"Aight," David answers. "I'll bring over some rolls. I forgot to pick some up anyway."

Walking up the driveway to Sam's house, David all of a sudden hears a loud smoke detector.

"Oh, shit," he says.

He runs up the steps, skipping half of them and swings open the front door. "Damn, girl, what you burning up?" He can barely see through the thick cloud of smoke, but he can see Sam standing on a chair with a broom in her hand trying to stab the smoke detector dead.

David laughs.

"I got this," David says. He grabs the asparagus lying on the counter, washes them off and begins to prepare the meal. "Looks like I'm going to have to teach you a thing or two, shorty."

Sam hits his arm and stands beside him as he throws a piece of butter in the pan.

David reaches down and kisses her. "I love you, Sam," he says staring deep into her eyes.

Sam smiles. "I love you too."

Thirty minutes later, David has whipped up some fresh garlic mashed potatoes and baked a perfect medium T-bone steak with fresh asparagus on the side. They take their food to her room and enjoy conversation while the rain beats down on the roof.

"So what kind of car you want, Sam?" David asks while chewing on a piece of steak.

"I told you I don't want you buying me a car."

"That wasn't the question."

Sam sighs. "I want a Pink Range Rover."

David almost chokes on his garlic bread.

"Okay, okay."

David chews on his steak. He thinks about his plans of buying her a new car. *Yeah, she gon' love that.* He then takes another bite, savoring the fatty meat that is swimming in A1 sauce. He lets out a chuckle. *She really gonna flip when I show her my acceptance letter to college.*

"What are you laughing about?" Sam asks.

"Nothing."

David smiles at her, still chewing on the meat. *Yeah. Just wait.*

After their meal, David goes home. But then in the middle of the night, he finds himself right back in her bed. He has nightmares almost every night about the violent whippings he'd get when he was younger and Sam's warm body is his only remedy. It never fails. Every time he holds her in his arms, he sleeps peacefully.

Even though David sometimes sleeps in her bed, they never have sex.

"I want to wait until I'm married. You know, stay pure for my husband," Sam says when they get caught up in heavy kissing. At first, David didn't mind. He accepted it for what it was and decided that maybe it would be the best thing. But over time, it got harder and harder. Matter of fact, it was killing him. He'd get to touching her soft skin and raking his fingers through her silky hair, and he'd be so turned on that he'd have to leave.

"You are beautiful, smart, and driven out of this world. Why wouldn't I want to make love to you?" he'd say in his defense.

Somehow, the girls at school picked up on it. They knew that Sam was not giving it up. They jumped at every opportunity to take advantage of the situation.

One day, Sam had left for a week to go to Kentucky for her "It Takes a Village" mentoring program, while David was at school late in his culinary vocational class.

"What's up, D?" Trinity said as she strutted past David.

David's eyes wandered around the beautiful girl's body. He couldn't help but to look at her short skirt, her thick legs and immediately could imagine what it would be like to be inside of her. Like an Etch pad, he shook his head and the thoughts scrambled away. "I can't do this," he said, while viciously kneading the dough on the table.

Trinity smiled, knowing the affects she had on him. She slid her butt on David and wiggled it around his crouch.

Usually when Trinity does her "I want you" dance, David pushes her away. But that time was different. David hadn't seen or heard from Sam in a while. It was becoming harder and harder to wrestle down his manhood.

Before long, David was standing at Trinity's front door. Even then, he was still fighting within himself. "Just one time," he said.

While waiting nervously, he looked around. Deep down, he wanted something to happen, someone to stop him. But all he saw was trees waving, the squirrels dodging cars in search for their next nut, and the clouds that seemed to be giving him a thumbs up.

Waving her hips from side to side, Trinity slowly opened the door. The thoughts of turning back instantly disappeared. He stared at her plump breasts and bit his lips.

Her lure was too powerful; she smelled like French vanilla ice cream. Her words were soft and sensuous. His heart was beating fast and his body was becoming weak.

"I'm ready for whatever," she said, whispering in his ear and biting it, too.

"You got a rubber?" he whispered back.

With a seductive voice, she whispered, "We don't need one."

David pushed the girl off of him.

"What?" he said. "We don't need one?"

"You little nasty ass hoe." Disappointed at her and even more in himself, he shook his head all the way back to the car.

Tucked deep down in David's pocket was a condom, but she failed the test.

"Naw, I'm cool." He laughs at himself. "Yeah. I'm cool."

After hearing those words slip out of her mouth so easily, David never thought about stepping out on Sam again. Getting some was no longer appealing.

He turned up his music, allowing the bass to calm his nerves. "Girls are doing anyone without protecting themselves and not caring what they sharing. Sam is well worth the wait," he said as he sped off.

"So, you stopped the drug thing?" Sam asks as they lay down together in her room.

"Yeah, I been stopped smoking weed," he answers, trying to sway away from the real question.

Sam smacks her lips, "You know what I mean. Do you still sell drugs?"

"Why we always have to talk about what I'm doing? Why don't we talk about what you doing? Are you... um... you know... washing yo ass."

They both laugh. David reaches up and kisses her. His warm sensuous kiss calms her down. "Listen, I'm almost out the game. I just needed to stack up so that I can get some things I need. Give me a little more time."

He kisses her again, but this time even more intense and intentional.

The room gets hot and Sam breaks away as usual, leaving that awkward pause between the two.

"Eh, you still looking for them journals?" David asks Sam.

Sam shakes her head. "Naw."

David looks at her sad face. He knows it is a touchy subject, but as always, he finds a way to make her frown turn into a smile.

"I'm going to come over here tomorrow. We're going to find those journals. I think if you had them, you would be a lot happier. You're too damn beautiful to be all sad and shit."

His words make her fall in love with him even more. Her heart beats fast. When David said he would do something, he always came through.

"We gon' find them. I promise," he says.

David looks at his cell phone. It reads 8:23.

"I gotta get outta here. I"ll call you in a couple of hours, aight?"

"Aight."

They kiss and then David leaves. When he gets to the sidewalk, right before he is about to hop into the car, he looks up to her window and smiles. "Damn, I love that girl."

He drives off thinking about how lucky he is and how his life is finally looking on the up and up.

Sam, who is still sitting up on her bed, ruffling the corners of her braided pillow is contemplating if she should start looking for the journals again. She had looked everywhere. However, there is only one place in the whole house she hadn't ever looked. A place that she had never gone and never had the desire to go. *I'm just going to go up there, look around and I'll be back down in a quick second.* She sits there for ten minutes talking herself into the idea. *I need to go to the attic. I have to find those journals.*

Sam jumps out of her bed and heads into her mother's room in search for the keys. She knows they have to be somewhere in her drawer; she had seen them there a couple of times over the years. Determined to find them, she doesn't allow anything to distract her. Not the broken crack pipes hiding in the corner of the drawer, not the syringe needles lying on the bed, and not even the blood droplets on her mother's scrambled sheets. She is focused; she doesn't want to allow her mind to wonder. Soon she succeeds at her goal. She finds what she is looking for - the silver keys that could possibly be the key to her destiny.

CHAPTER TWENTY TWO

S am slowly slides the key into the hole. She turns the knob, and without any assistance, the door eerily squeaks open by itself. A lingering stench of sex and must hits her in the face. It is thick and smothering.

As she climbs up the dusty steps, she squints her eyes to adjust to the darkness. And when they do, she is shocked at what she sees.

On the floor are rows of small, cot-like mattresses, lined from the top of the steps to the end of the room. Thin, dingy colored sheets are rigged with homemade string to close off different areas of the attic. She immediately holds her stomach and gasps for air.

What in the... I can't believe this. She shakes her head and keeps moving.

Forcing her mouth closed so she doesn't inhale the dust that's drifting in the air, she reminds herself that she is on a mission. She scans the room and quickly finds a door. It's short and wide. The only door in the attic. Like a game of hopscotch, Sam skips and jumps over mattress after mattress until finally she is in the dark closet. A string hanging from a naked light bulb brushes up against her face. She tugs at it, but nothing happens; it just swings in the air. Determined to turn it on, she yanks it down.

Finally there is light.

Boxes. Yes! Boxes, Sam thinks, as her heart races with excitement. A smile breaks through and if it wasn't for the smell and dust floating in the air, she would open her mouth and sigh with relief.

There is an array of boxes, all sizes and shapes. Some bent up, some standing tall just waiting to be opened. She immediately gets to work. Every box she opens seems to be bringing her closer to her lost treasure. Sam grabs another box, stabs it with the key, runs it down the middle of the tape and pulls away the flaps like it's a competition. Nothing but trash. She tosses it and moves on to the next.

In the far corner, a small box catches her eye. It is sitting under an old dusty table. On top of the table is an old antique sewing machine. A sad feeling comes over her body. Taking baby steps

toward the sewing machine that still has thread and cloth draped within it, she closes her eyes to imagine her mother using it. She imagines her beautiful smile, her soft voice calling her name and even holding her hand as they skip to the park. Sam touches it and smoothes her hand along the neck of the sewing machine. She caresses the cloth and then holds it up to her nose in hopes of getting even a hint of scent of her. Overwhelmed with sadness, she shakes her head. *I have to find those journals. I just have to.* Sam reaches down for the box and tears it open. Dipping her hand inside, she pulls out a necklace. As soon as she sees it, she smiles. Hanging from the chain is a beautiful gold charm. It has the letter S engraved on it. Sam holds the charm up to her lips and kisses it. She then stuffs it in her pocket so she can get back to searching for the journals.

In some boxes she finds pictures of herself and her mother and even some of her father. However, there is one picture that stands out and brings her to tears. As she holds the picture in her hands, her eyes wander from her father's sharp black suit to her mother's elegant white dress with a train wrapped around her on the floor. *Mom, you were so beautiful.* Sam combs her hair, imagining that it is her mother's hair. She then rubs her finger along the picture. She smiles at the happy toddler that is swaddled in her mother's arms as they take a family picture on their wedding day.

All of a sudden, a strange noise startles her. She drops the picture. It waves in the air and then lands on the dusty wooden floor. She hears a bunch of voices, a lot of commotion at the bottom of the steps and then people running up to the attic. She quickly and quietly shuts the door and then kneels down. She takes short, shallow breaths, but it's hard to control the force of the air as her lungs pick up speed.

One man after another, she watches them walk into the attic. Then comes a couple of women. She can't see too much from the small crack in the door, but the glimpse that she does get disturbs her.

She can see her stepmother's long wig and then her naked body. She sees her kneeling down holding a man's penis while the other man yanks on her hair. It happens so fast, her mind can't comprehend it all. She knows what is happening, but watching her mother being jerked every which a way makes her stomach uneasy.

In the distance are other voices, moans, smacks and men making orders like they are at McDonald's. "Turn around...bend over...yeah, like that, stop fucking moving," they aggressively and so easily yell. Her nausea starts to ease. Instead of feeling sick inside, her adrenaline is taking over her senses. Her body is getting ready for war. She hears a loud smack and her eyes dart back to Courtney. She is stretched across the floor, holding her face and whimpering in pain. Standing over her are two men. They are laughing and watching her.

"Get up!" one of the men yell.

When the man looks up, Sam can clearly see his face. She gasps for air and bolts out of the room.

"Jacob!" Sam yells. It is Daniel's father. She yells it so loud, the name echoes through the attic and out of the attic window.

"You fucking…" Sam is so mad that she doesn't even realize that she is out of her hiding place and within inches of Jacob's chest.

Jacob just stands there, shocked. Not only is he embarrassed, but seeing her look at his pale naked body sends an electric shock through every limb, making him stiff as a board. Sam turns to the other man.

"Tommy?"

She recognizes his partner, his little sidekick. The man that used to ride past in his police car and pass out candy to David, Daniel, and Sam as kids. He too looks shocked and confused. Then Sam looks down at her mother. She is slurring words. She is high, but trying to fight it. She is trying to come back to reality, but Sam can tell it is a struggle.

Suddenly, the door downstairs slams hard against the wall. Slams so hard it sounds as if the door knob has torn a hole through it. Boots are stomping up the steps like the swat team busting a drug house.

"Give me everything you got, money, dope. Give me the mothafuckin' chains off your neck. I don't care, I want everything," the masked man orders.

The other two men with dark masks march around the room. They are holding black Glocks, waving them at everyone and anyone who dares to move. Jacob and his partner are defenseless.

With no gun, they can do nothing but kneel down like little girls with their hands up in the air.

Sam, on the other hand, stands tall. She doesn't care about the robbery as much as she is thinking about her mother and the state she is in. The men start tossing up mattress after mattress, going through pocket after pocket of abandoned clothes and just tearing up everything in sight.

In the middle of all of the commotion, one of the men stops abruptly and stares at Sam. He is the leader of the group; the one giving most of the orders. He tilts his head like he recognizes her. Grabbing her arm, he snatches her up and throws her into the dark closet.

"Eh, get my back," he yells to one of the gunman. He walks into the dusty closet, shuts the door and quickly yanks her pants off.

"No, please, don't. Don't. No!" she begs.

She yells so loud she can feel a burning sensation in her throat. Fighting him, punching him, digging her fingernails into his skin, she tries to stop him, but it is to no avail. He opens her legs and thrusts himself inside of her. She screams in pain, and fights as hard as her strength will allow her until suddenly, her mind drifts away. She can't feel too much of anything. But then, something brings her back to consciousness. She can hear a faint ring. It is the telephone ringing downstairs.

"David!" she screams. "Daaavid!"

The man punches her in her mouth, forcing her head to turn. She doesn't say another word. She then hears her mother yelling for them to stop and then yelling for Jacob to do something. He does nothing. He just allows it to happen.

Sam closes her eyes, waiting for him to finish. Violently - without any regard to her pain - he continues thrusting himself in and out of her. Finally he jerks one last time, gets up, and leaves. She is left there, throbbing, bleeding and wavering in and out of consciousness.

As soon as the men leave, Sam's stepmother rushes into the room and so does Jacob. Jacob's figure is blurry to Sam as he is hovering over her. She can see his head nodding. He is giving Courtney a sign, a sign that Sam can't make out.

Courtney holds her daughter's body, attempting to soothe her.

Sam lies there for a second, allowing her mother's naked body to rest on hers, and then she suddenly gets up. She stumbles out of the darkness and wobbles into the now lit and empty room. Everyone is gone. Everyone. Some even left their things. Courtney tries helping Sam. Sam just yanks away. She is mad. She is angry and she can't believe what her mother was telling her as she rocked her like a baby. "You can't tell anyone. No one will believe you. It happened to me. It will be okay. It's over now."

Sam is numb, but she sure as hell isn't dumb. She knows that her mother is just trying to cover it up to save her and Jacob's ass. She wants to punch her mother in the face, toss her ass down the steps, and stomp on her head until she takes her last breath.

"Get the fuck away from me," Sam says in pain. She limps down the steps and then into the bathroom. When Sam gets the strength to look into the mirror, she sees her busted lip and a cut across her face. It takes everything in her to not just punch the glass and cut her wrist. As she takes a shower, she tries scrubbing every part of her body, but can never achieve a clean feeling. *That's it. I'm done. I can't take it anymore. I can't take my life. I've tried. But I can't do it.*

Her tears stream down her face along with the warm drips of water falling to the tub.

Exhausted, confused, and still feeling dirty inside, she covers herself in her blanket and hides. Hour after hour, she goes through a cycle of crying, yelling, and thoughts of swallowing a handful of pills or hanging herself. She replays the act as if it's a movie. *Am I fucking dreaming? I can't believe this is real. Why? Who?* With too many emotions running around deep inside, Sam closes her eyes and fights her thoughts to go to sleep.

The next day, Sam finds herself unable to get out of bed. Not just because of the pain inside of her body, but also from the heaviness of her heart. *I've done everything I was supposed to do. I do everything right. I don't steal, I don't do drugs, why me?*

Her eyes are swollen from crying and from being hit and her legs feel like bricks when she tries to move them to get out of bed.

The doorbell rings. It's David. Her heart feels like it's about to explode, it's beating so hard. She rolls out of her bed, jumps up to the window, and yells from the window. "I'm sick. I'll call you." She ducks behind the curtain so he can't see her bruised face.

"You good?" he yells back. "You need anything?"

"Yeah, I'm straight," she says, trying to control every word in her voice.

David shrugs his shoulders and Sam watches him drive away.

A couple of days pass and David has still not seen her face.

"No, you can't come over," Sam says, frustrated and trying to rattle her voice.

David sighs. "For real, Sam. It's really that deep. You acting like you have to be quarantined or something."

"Oh, nothing like that, David. I just really need some time to myself. I'm on my period and it's heavy, I have cramps out—"

David interrupts, "All right. All right. I ain't tryna hear all that. Just holla at me when you get better, okay? I left you something on the porch. I love you."

Sam cracks a smile. "I love you, too."

As soon as Sam gets off the phone, she relaxes her tired face from having to force a smile throughout the conversation.

Once she is up to it, she goes downstairs and finds the "thing" that David left for her.

It puts a genuine smile on her face. Still in her pajamas, she opens up the Tupperware and instantly the delicious smelling steam makes her mouth water. "Homemade chicken noodle soup. Only David," she says with a smile. She looks out to the street. She almost catches a figure behind a bush, but it moves before she can focus on it.

"She doesn't look all that sick to me," David says, watching her skip back into the house. He shakes his head, bites his lip and then walks back home.

Once Sam finally decides to go back to school, everyone including David is surprised to see her look so worn down. They are asking her all kinds of questions. Even her teachers are concerned. Sam doesn't say much, though. She shrugs them off and gradually begins to act as if nothing had ever happened.

David still feels deep down inside that something is wrong. He can tell by the silent moments, the awkward gazing, and the lack of conversation. He knows she is always a serious person, but never *that* serious.

"Babe, what's up with you?" David asks while sitting on the porch of his house.

Sam turns her attention to an ant that is carrying another dead ant. "Why can't people be like ants? Why can't they just have each other's back instead of always trying to keep each other down?"

David looks at Sam's sad eyes. "Why you trying to change the subject, Sam?"

"I'm not. I'm just saying. Why is it that we can't work together in this world? I don't know how many times I have seen the smallest ants work together to build huge mounds." She looks at David. "This world could be like that, but we are all too busy looking out for self."

"Sam! What's wrong with you? You making me nervous. Did something happen?"

Sam gets up from the steps, not saying a word. She walks a couple of feet away from him and looks him directly in the face.

"I told your dumb ass I was okay. Leave me the fuck alone."

David's body tenses as he doesn't know what to do.

Sam starts yelling again. "You know what's wrong with me?" she pats her chest. "You wanna know what's wrong with me? You!" Leaning toward him, she pokes the air with her finger. "You bring me down. You don't have a dream. You don't have a job. You're fucking worthless."

David's face twists as he is caught completely off guard.

A man walking past who witnessed the whole thing looks at the anger in David's face. He sees him about to blow up. "Don't do it, chief. Don't do it. Just let her go."

David looks over at the man as if he were an angel. Instead of saying another word, he just gets up and walks into his house.

Weeks later in class, Sam sits in her usual chair a couple of seats from the front and David sits in the back. David watches her as she is slouching down in her chair with her hand holding her mouth.

"Something ain't right. I swear," he says.

All of a sudden, David sees Sam grab her stomach. She twists in her chair and then jerks her head over her desk and hurls up something terrible. Her body gyrates back and forth as she unloads chunks of chicken nuggets and purplish contents onto the floor.

David shakes his head. "I can't believe it. I fucking can't believe it," he shouts.

"That girl is pregnant. I know she is," one girl says as Sam lays her head down onto the desk. "Those symptoms right there, oh, I know 'bout that."

A couple of missed days of school later, Sam starts withdrawing from everyone. The teachers are trying to talk to her about her slipping grades and the principal tries talking to her stepmother.

"Look, I just want to finish my junior year," she tells the prying counselor.

Soon, Sam herself knows something is wrong. But still she refuses to take a pregnancy test. *I can't be pregnant. I just can't be.*

However, after a second missed period, she can't deny it any longer. She goes to the store, buys a pregnancy test and to her disappointment, the girls at school are right. She is definitely pregnant.

The news to David is horrifying. "Damn. I thought you were different. You a hoe just like everybody else around here. What is it, something in the damn water?" he says, trying to conceal his hurt.

"Who was it?" he says.

Like a child being chastised by their mother, Sam looks up at David in shame. She hesitates. "A dude I met at the mall."

"Just some random dude, huh?"

David clenches his teeth and narrows his eyes at Sam. He balls up his fist and moves it from side to side. He fights back his anger, swallowing it and then walks out of the house. It is the last time Sam sees him. He literally disappears. He drops out of school and never returns.

CHAPTER TWENTY THREE

Senior Year

"**S**amantha Lariyah Johnson."

The sound of her name signaling it is time for her to walk across the stage is exuberating. Sam tightens her grip around her diploma, pauses on stage with the bright lights shining on her equally bright smile and scans the audience. In the front row, she spots Amina.

Amina is yelling "Sam" so loud and so long after the applause that the principal has to wait until she sits back down. Even then, the applause starts roaring through the auditorium for Sam.

Sam takes in the praise as she takes in a deep breath. She looks at her son. He is standing tall on her friend's lap, mimicking claps, smiling, and showing off his one and only tooth. "We did it," she mouths with tears welling up in her eyes.

After watching the other graduates snap pictures with their family, Sam finds herself scanning the auditorium one last time for two people - two people who she had loved all of her life - her stepmother Courtney and David. Sadly neither of them are there. She has not heard from David since she told him she was pregnant over a year ago and her stepmother said she would try to make it, but when it comes to Courtney, she never gets her hopes up.

Sam twirls her straw around the glass of iced tea, studying the ice cubes as they swim around. While sitting in a booth waiting for her food, she listens to the other graduates talk about studying abroad and how they will spend their summer being free to do what they please.

"I will be leaving for an internship in Washington D.C. soon," a girl sitting across from her says. Another blurts out, "Ohio State. Here I come. Yeah, boo!"

They go on and on about their plans.

"So, Sam," Veronica, the snobbiest of the group says, "How does it feel to be a mother with diverted dreams?"

Sam stops twirling the straw. She stares at the pale girl for a second, debating whether or not she should swing on her or walk out a classy woman. She stands up and slams her palms onto the table. Making sure the girl reads her eyes just as much as hears her words, she says, "Best believe, nothing will divert me from my dreams."

Sam walks out of the diner with her head held high and quickly swipes the one tear she couldn't hold back. It took a lot for Sam to keep her composure. She remembers that Amina said it's a part of growing up, using her fight for the right reasons. That's the only thing that saved that poor girl from an ass whipping.

As she walks through the projects, ducking under clotheslines and walking through walkways to cross over to her apartment, she thinks about the past year. She thinks about how long it took her to step into the dimly lit welfare office. How, when she was younger, she vowed she'd never be dependent on government assistance; she'd witnessed the horrible affects. "It's evil," Amina would say to her. "Receiving free money can cause you to become lax, lax when it comes to your dreams, and it can make you get used to accepting crumbs over going out there to get all the world has to offer." That thought takes her to another, the last time she had a deep conversation with Amina.

"Sam. Stop crying," Amina said, lifting Sam's head up from the wooden table. "Think about your history. Think about what your ancestors had to endure just to survive. Picture the slave women with their babies on their scarred backs as they picked cotton from sunup to sundown. With blistered fingers and barely enough to eat, they remained strong. Why the hell can't you rock Jeremy to sleep in one hand and hold a book in the other? I did." She placed her hand over Sam's round belly. "I know your friends are shopping for wall decorations and lamps for their dorms while you're out here buying Pampers and formula and working while they partying. But guess what? You have an advantage. You have something to fight for."

Knock. Knock.

Sam stops pouring milk into the plastic bottle and peeks her head into the living room.

Knock. Knock.

It is not a friendly knock - more like an "open up this door for me right now" kind of knock. She looks at her baby, who is sitting on the carpet clenching down on his teething ring, lips and cheeks covered with slobber, grabs him and carries him to his crib. She then snatches the bat that is sitting in the corner and grips it as if she is next to bat at a baseball game. Peeking through the tiny peep hole, she can't see anything. She pulls her curtains a little to see if anyone is hiding. There is no one. It scares her. After a while, she decides to just open the door and scan the perimeter.

As soon as she opens the door, a floating pink balloon with its string attached to a brown box appears. Immediately, she smiles. She quickly grabs it. Once it's safe and she is in the house, she slides her hand under the envelope's lips to get to the card. The card that has teddy bears and a heart on it reads, "I am proud of you." She checks to see if there is any money, but nothing is there. She even turns the envelope upside down, but again, nothing.

Next, Sam grabs the box. She peels the edges of the tape, rips it off, and opens the four flaps. Her eyes widen. In the background she hears her baby crying, but at this point it seems so faint, she ignores him. She reaches inside and pulls out a stash of money. At first the sight of the money scares her. However, when she sees a piece of paper with David's name, she knows it came from a person who would never cause her harm.

The words "I don't have much to say" are scribbled out on a sheet of paper and up under it are the words, "Spend it wisely." That was it. No address. No nothing. Sitting on her lap, is a box full of money and there is no way that she can call and thank him.

Sam looks up at her dream board, a new one that her mentor made her create while she was pregnant. On it is a picture of a cheerful professor with a child running around a large yard, and it has a range rover that she colored over with a pink marker. *Those are my dreams.* She looks down at the money and she knows what to do with it. She would do with it what she does to almost every cent that passes through her hands. Save it.

A lot of the young girls talk about her in the neighborhood. They talk about her clothes because she shuffles the same thrift store outfits week by week. She does her own hair - a ponytail is just fine - and she drives a beat up car that she has to climb through the passenger side just to get out of.

Who am I trying to impress? We all broke. Why would I waste my money on a hundred dollar pair of shoes when that can go toward a book for college? I'm not about to get comfortable here. This isn't my home. As she walks around her empty apartment and when she lies down to sleep on a couple of blankets on the floor, it reminds her of what she doesn't have. It motivates her to go out there and go get it.

"Hey, Ma! Did Raymond stop by there today?"

"Oh, Raymond. What a sweet young man. Yes, he did." Tara says. "Thanks for the money. You just don't know how much that helps. You truly are a blessing, son. I plan on coming out there so I can see you. I miss you," Tara says while stirring a pot of greens.

"Don't. I mean… you don't have to. I'll be out in two weeks. But, um, Ma, that's my time. I have one minute left. I love you. I'll call you next week," David says.

"I love you, too. Bye, baby."

After getting off of the phone with his mother, David becomes bothered. He was sad while he was actually on the phone, but he waits until he makes it to his bunk to actually show it. It's been a year since he was a free man and it still hasn't gotten any easier saying goodbye to his mother.

A whole year. Wasted. Just because of money. He shakes his head. *KG told me. Sam told me.* As he sits on the edge of his mattress, one thought leads to another. He closes his eyes and allows his mind to take him back. Back to a time when things were going so good in his life.

"David!" Sam said loudly in the quiet restaurant. "Get the stuff off of your face."

"You want it off, you have to lick it off," David joked with BBQ sauce dripping from the corners of his mouth.

"Ew. You so nasty," Sam said.

"Go 'head. Lick it."

Sam didn't know what to do. There she was in a fine dining restaurant with her boyfriend acting stupid, embarrassing her and she can't seem to stop laughing. She can't even keep a straight face while telling him to stop.

"Please, David, you're embarrassing me."

"Lick it then." David grabbed her hand and gently pulled it toward his face.

Sam wiggled and tried to pull away but couldn't. David succeeded. He pulled her finger all the way to his lips.

"Ah!" Sam screamed.

All of a sudden everyone in the restaurant was staring at them both. Everyone was dressed up in their suits and gowns, while Sam and David were in street clothes.

"Sorry, but I'm going to have to ask you two to leave," the waiter said, hurrying to their table.

Even when the skinny man came over to the table, Sam was still dying laughing.

"I paid just like everyone else. I ain't leaving shit," David snapped back.

"Please for the sake of our other patrons, keep it down," the man pleads.

"I ain't doing shit," David said as the waiter walked away.

By this time Sam had gotten herself together and calmed David's hot head down.

Remembering that moment just makes him laugh. It is too funny not to. He looks around at the four concrete walls closing in on him and realizes he is still in jail. Bars and cramped quarters. He closes his eyes and allows himself to take another flight away from bondage.

He remembers one day walking up to Daniel. Daniel was bouncing a basketball on the sidewalk and talking to Sam. It was a hot summer day and Daniel had just gotten a fat check from the insurance company.

"Yep, I'm going to North Academy. It's for my people. It sure beats going to that ghetto place that y'all call a school," Daniel said to Sam.

David looked at him. He didn't like the expression Daniel wore on his face, how he talked with his head tilted up higher than necessary; he didn't like the way his words came out. David just shook his head and let his girl talk.

"I don't care. I don't care what school I go to. As long as I can become a professor."

Sam said it with such grace and confidence.

"Yeah right, more like a nurse. The doctor's hoe."

David calmly replied, "What you say?"

Daniel twisted his lips to say, "You heard me."

However, it was too late.

Ba-bop. With his signature two piece, David knocked Daniel to the concrete. Before he even fell, Daniel was already sleeping. Sam covered her mouth, looked at David, and then looked back at Daniel.

"That's what you get," she yelled.

David stepped over him and yelled in his ear as loud as humanly possible.

"You betta respect ma girl!"

Sam and David both walked away while the sun shined on Daniel's busted nose and lip.

David was proud to take up for the most beautiful girl on the block and Sam was proud he did.

Opening his eyes back up, David shakes his head and laughs again.

"What you down there laughing at?" his bunkie, Kareem, asks cautiously.

"Oh, memories. Just the good ol' days."

His roomie listens while David tells him a story.

"I remember when I was at this dude's house and he pulled out a box of crack."

"Whoa!" Kareem interrupts.

"Yeah," David says. "I was only about ten or eleven years old. Now that was almost an ass whippin' I would have never forgotten about. Dude's momma was cracked out by the time I was thirteen. I mean out here hard. Then dude got some money, started selling, getting his product from a dude in Florida...a professor, can you believe that? And the next thing I knew, he was on that shit. Not crack, but meth. It was just all bad. That's the drug game for you, though, it never ends good. For nobody."

"You say, dude had got some money?" Kareem asks.

"Yeah, his granddad got killed and left him with a lot of money. Dude out here stuntin'." The bunkie pauses for a second. "You talking 'bout Daniel?"

"Yeah, why? You know him?" David asks.

"Cause me and Daniel used to go stickin' people up. Taking shit, everything we could get. Then he started trippin'. He was wildin' out, and I couldn't even fuck with him like that anymore."

Proud that he had something in common with one of the toughest inmates, Kareem couldn't wait to get on David's good side.

The man sits up in his thin mattress, rubs his hands together and says, "Man, do I got a story for you."

CHAPTER TWENTY FOUR

K areem sits up in his thin mattress, anxious to tell his story. He assumes that by telling the story, he can maybe get some street cred. Then, perhaps, David wouldn't be so intimidating.

"I can remember it just like it was yesterday. Fucking around with Daniel's crazy ass. We were all chillin' in his living room, eating pizza and watching *The Wire*. It was me and my li'l brother."

Immediately, David starts imagining the whole thing happen. He listens so intently he is able to place himself right there in Daniel's living room, a place he remembers so vividly.

"We were both bored and broke. Daniel was different. Like you said, he had money. A lot of times he'd have thousands of dollars stashed in his room just waiting for the right person to come and steal it. He was dumb. Other than that, Daniel was cool. — Well, at first. He had the money, the guns, and when we rolled with him, we knew we were going to make a come up."

"That night, the plan went down a little differently. Daniel acted normal, laughing and joking with us, just chillin'. Then all of a sudden, he changed. The only thing I could guess made him flip like that was that his father had just left the house. That's when he just flipped out, like he was possessed. My brother looked at me and I looked at my brother. I looked at Daniel and saw that he was plotting. He wasn't thinking about just the normal stick up and I'm out. If I ever saw evil in a person, it was that night. Just out the blue, Daniel says to us, 'Eh, I know this place that we can stickup. It's a house just down the street that my father used to take me to...

I mean he used to go up in there and leave my ass in the car. I'd just play my games and wait until he got back. Then, one day I found out what it was. It's gonna be the perfect stickup.' Me and Alex was thrown off. We ain't know what kind of house he was talking about. Daniel had already planned it out, but he wanted to move fast. He wanted to hurry up and get the money and be back before it got too late. Me and my brother was down. We needed the money, we were hurting. But Daniel, on the other hand, he just did the shit for fun."

David, who is still quiet, is taking in every single word of his roommate.

"We get there, and it seems like everything was going wrong. For one, when we get up to the attic, we see his father up there, butt naked with some hoe on the ground, wiggling around and shit. Who would want to see their daddy's ass out? For real? It freaked me out and that wasn't even my damn daddy. Daniel wanted his daddy to watch. We got the money, jewelry, and some dope and was about to head out. Then Daniel saw a girl. I had seen her, too. Who wouldn't? She was beautiful, big brown eyes, looking like Pocahontas."

Kareem takes a second to think about her face.

"I mean the girl looked like she came straight up out a movie. Fine as hell."

David instantly sits up. He has to catch himself from tipping off Kareem. His eyes are getting tight and his muscles are naturally contracting. He has to really control himself at this point.

"The next thing I knew, Daniel had thrown the girl in this closet and was going in. We could hear the whole thing. He was wildin' out, fucking crazy. She was screaming, yelling, and kicking the door."

David's chest starts rising up to its full air capacity and quickly falls back down. His heart pounds and pounds until it feels like it's trying to come out. He is fuming with rage, but again, he swallows it to hear the rest of the story.

"The screaming stopped when Daniel punched her a couple of times. It was crazy. Then out of nowhere, she called out a name. She was screaming it for a while. She screamed—"

Kareem suddenly stops. His eyes roll up. He silently mouths the word "shit."

It dawns on him that it was David she was screaming for. He quickly goes back to the story.

"She screamed, um, Tony. Yeah, that was the name. And after that, I bust in there and got Daniel up out of there. The whole thing went bad fast."

"That's it?" David asks as calmly as possible.

"Yeah. That's about it," Kareem stutters, carefully lying back down on the mattress.

Kareem closes his eyes, but he can feel the room getting hotter and hotter. Kareem can feel the fear rise inside of his body. Bullets of sweat start to force their way through his skin.

It gets so hot, he thinks he feels another body standing next to him. He's afraid to open his eyes. "I know this dude ain't standing next to me. I hope his big ass ain't standing next to me," Kareem whispers to himself.

Kareem opens his eyes. David is standing there, staring back at him. For a second, David studies him, contemplating what he is going to do next, but the dumb look on Kareem's face pisses him off even more.

Before Kareem can move, David grabs Kareem's neck with one hand and slings him onto the floor. He starts stomping his head. Every muscle in David's body is crashing down on Kareem's body, some of the blows missing while the others landing. He is so angry, he loses it. His intention was to just hit him once, but once he started, he couldn't stop. Blood splatters on the wall, the toilet, and soon a pool of blood starts spilling on the floor.

Kareem stops moving. The sight of blood scares David. He immediately stops and pulls Kareem back up. Bloody and almost unconscious, Kareem struggles to fully wake up. His head is waving from side to side, freaking David out even more.

Panicked, David cups some water from the toilet and then throws it on him. "Wake up. Wake up," David whispers.

Kareem finally comes to.

Once David realizes he is okay, he feels a sense of relief. *I got two more weeks. I can't fuck this up.*

Kareem stumbles to get up. David just watches him. He watches him splash water in his face and wipe the blood from his head. When he is done, Kareem's eyes wander everywhere. Everywhere but on David. He looks at the floor, the wall, and then climbs onto the mattress. He doesn't say a word.

After a couple of minutes have passed, something tells David to say something. Usually, he wouldn't, but something is nagging him.

"Eh, Kareem," he says.

Kareem hesitates. He wipes the blood from his mouth. "Yeah."

"I know I just whooped your ass and all, but I got a question for you."

"Yeah," Kareem answered.

"Why didn't you stop it? Why would you let a punk dude like Daniel rape a girl and you not stop it? I mean. What if that was your mother?"

Kareem is silent for a second. He clears his throat and then says, "I wouldn't fucking care if it was my mother."

David is thrown back and getting angry again. *What kind of dude would say that about their moms? I'd kill someone. I'd kill for my mother.*

"My mother left me when I was born. I was a crack baby. I gives a fuck about my mother because she didn't give a fuck about me."

At that point, David's heart drops. It is like deja vu. He can hear Sam when she would say, "Think about where the child of that crack head you sold drugs to gon' be. Did you think about who that child is going to grow up and become? Who he gonna kill because his mother was strung out and he feels alone and unloved?"

David had finally got it. It had finally clicked. He is now living the effects of the seeds he had planted.

It makes him feel even worse. It is on his shoulders now. He feels responsible for what happened to Sam. *I can't believe I treated her like that. I can't believe I let this shit happen. And she was calling my name. I wasn't there for her. I just left her.* It becomes too much for him to bear. He is so angry. The feeling of guilt is making his eyes swell and tears are running down his face. He can't wipe them away fast enough.

Shaking his leg and trying to keep his composure, he closes his eyes and prays. He prays that somehow, someway, he can get rid of the anger. If only he can erase the pain, then maybe he can spare Daniel's life. He shakes his head again. *I am just not that damn strong. That mothafucka is gonna to have to die.*

Every night since he found out about what happened, David wakes up with nightmares. Some nights he dreams of Sam getting raped and he not being able to help her, while other nights he dreams that he is smashing Daniel's face into the concrete. There is no getting around it. He can't shake the screams, the images, and guilt that fills his heart when he thinks about what happened to the only one he has ever truly loved.

He thinks about writing Sam, apologizing, to ease his mind. But stomaching the words, "Rape," "I'm sorry for not being there," or even, "Daniel," are beyond his capabilities.

Raymond pulls up to the prison in a silver 911 Porsche waiting for his best friend to finally leave the gates of hell. He's wearing a striped Nautica button down with a pair of Nautica khakis and in his hand he is holding a Blackberry. Focused on a text message that his secretary has sent him, he doesn't even realize David has just been set free.

"Raymond!" David yells, walking down the sidewalk.

"D!" Raymond yells back, almost dropping his phone. Raymond watches his friend and smiles. He's playing it cool like he doesn't want to look weird running into another man's arms, but as soon as D gets close enough, he speed walks, and gives his brother a hug.

"Man, it feels good to be free. I ain't never going back," David says.

"D, you said that last time."

"Yeah, that was because I ain't really believe Cathy and KG was going to really let me sit in there."

David waves his hands to the barb wires and the building. "Right here, this shit real. The hardest dude in there wish they can break up out of there."

"Where we to first?" Raymond asks while pulling out of the parking lot.

"Regal Projects."

"Regal Projects? I ain't going down there. Do you see what I'm driving?"

"Man, you always so damn scared."

"No, I'm smart," Raymond says, laughing.

"Aight then, just drop me at the station and I'll catch the bus down there."

"The bus? When was the last time you caught the damn bus? Why don't I just stop through your house so you can swoop up your ride?"

"I can't go there yet, I have some stops to make first."

David has a plan. Raymond has no idea and neither does anyone else. It is just the way he wants to keep it. When it comes to doing his dirty work, he wants to be the only one responsible for his own life. Too many times, he has witnessed his closest friends, and even sometimes family, snitching. He is not about to put his life in somebody else's hands.

Raymond doesn't ask any more questions. He just does what his friend asks. He pulls up to the train station, gives him a couple of dollars, and watches him get out of the car.

"I'll holla at you later, bruh."

"Fo sho."

"Ay!" David says, catching Raymond right before he pulls off. "Thanks, man. Thanks for holding me down and looking out for the fam. I—"

Suddenly, Raymond's phone rings; he ignores it.

"Yeah, but…"

The phone rings again. Raymond puts it on vibrate and signals for David to continue.

David sees that someone is trying to call him.

"Never mind, man. I'll just talk to you later."

"Aight."

Raymond pulls off.

David listens to the sweet sound of the Porsche, watches the smoke rush from its pipes and then runs to catch the next bus. While on the bus, he runs through his plan over and over again. He plays it in his head like a football player would be envisioning the play that will get him the winning touchdown. He is concentrating, focused. *I have to just see her one last time. I need to see that she is all right.*

David gets off of the bus. He walks to the corner store across the street from the apartment complex and then starts to wonder what he is going to say to her. He grabs a Black and Mild cigar, lights it and inhales deeply to calm his nerves. All of a sudden, he hears an engine. The kind of engine you don't normally hear in the hood.

David looks around the corner and sees a silver Porsche.

He looks at the car and immediately gets nervous. *Something got to be wrong for him to be coming here.*

David rubs his cigar on the concrete to deaden the fire and then jogs across the street toward Raymond, who is headed for Sam's house.

"What's up, Ray?" David yells.

Raymond looks flustered. He is stumbling over his words and is really in a hurry.

"D! KG just got shot. He in the hospital."

"What?"

David is confused. His body is slow to react to the bad news. Then a surge of urgency rushes through him. He jumps in the car and Raymond speeds out of the parking lot.

"Wait, wait. Slow down," David says.

Right when they are pulling out, Sam is pulling in. She looks him dead in his face. With her beautiful eyes and matured features, for a hot second, David's heart beats fast for her.

The glance is quick, but it is just enough. It is just enough to put the seal on Daniel's fate. The anger he had felt when he first heard the story came back to him as soon as he saw her face.

"Aight, you can go."

"You know she can't see you right?" Raymond warns.

"Yeah, I know. But I saw her."

Raymond zooms to the hospital as fast as his car can take him. Even a Porsche with its powerful engine can't be fast enough for David to see his big brother.

CHAPTER TWENTY FIVE

"**S**am!" the giggling kids call out.

Sam has just left work at the steel factory and hasn't even made it out of her car before seeing a bunch of kids crowding around her doorstep.

"What's up Johann, Shelly, and Raven?" she says while struggling to get her keys out of her purse.

"And who are you and you?" she says to two little girls with two short ponytails in their hair.

Sam looks at the growing crowd of kids waiting for a piece of candy and someone to talk to.

Once she finally cracks the door open, the kids rush in.

Well, I guess I'm going to have a full house tonight.

"Okay, kids. I am not going to just give you candy anymore. Y'all are going to have to earn it."

She looks at the kids, who are now sitting quietly on her floor. Some still have the same clothes on since the last time she saw them, while others are rocking the latest name brands.

None of it is important to her, though. All she cares about is putting a smile on their faces.

"I tell you what. Let me put Jeremy in his crib and then I have a little surprise for you."

The kids start to cheer. "Surprise! Surprise!"

"Shh. The baby is asleep."

"Okay. Okay," they loudly whisper, still jumping up and down like colorful jelly beans on the floor.

As Sam walks to the back, she can hear little giggles in the living room. She imagines them all looking around and waiting for her to come out at any minute. She is also anxious and ready to get back to them.

Sam comes walking in with a handful of books.

"Ahh, man," the kids moan.

"What. You don't like to read?"

"No!" they say disappointed.

"Well, if you want some candy and you want to keep coming over here for dinner for my famous sweet potato pie, then you're going to have to read."

Sam is excited. Book after book, she sits there and reads to them. She pauses, asks questions, and tries to relate the stories to their life. It is a hit.

To her surprise, the kids are really into it. They love hearing the stories. They love taking turns to act out the characters and even though they don't realize it, they enjoy the thought provoking questions she asks.

After a while, she discovers that their favorite part is when she gives them the opportunity to tell their own personal stories. For many of them, it is the only chance they have to talk about their feelings, their thoughts, and to actually feel like they are worthy of sharing them.

Thirty minutes pass and the kids start to get restless. They are ready for their candy. Sam passes out the assorted colored Starbursts and asks them what they think about coming back.

"Ohh, I wanna come back. I wanna come back," they say, jumping with the half chewed candy in their mouths.

"Stop jumping with that in your mouth," Sam says.

They immediately stop jumping.

It makes her smile. It makes her happy, the way she connects with the kids.

"What if, next time, we go to the library? That way, you guys can pick out your very own books?"

"Yay!" they all cheer.

One by one the kids skip out of her house and run to show off their candy. Sam feels prouder than ever. And even though they are gone, she is sure most will come back for dinner. In just a few short hours her floor will be covered with newspaper and little bodies will be wiggling around, stuffing their stomachs with a home cooked meal.

Sam looks up at her dream board hanging by a piece of tape on the wall. It is filled with her dreams, a Range Rover and a huge house with a couple of acres of green land. Suddenly, instead of seeing things that will make her happy, she sees a poster board full of magazine clippings of material things. After reading to the children and spending time with them, the material things seem so shallow to her.

What am I chasing? What am I going to get out of having a 60 thousand dollar car? A huge house for just me and my son?

All of a sudden Sam's dreams begin to change. All of the things she thought she needed in order to feel fulfilled don't matter to her anymore. She has stepped out of the illusion that she had been fed all of her life. From the TV shows to the commercials, to the billboards and the cosmetic aisles of cover up telling her what she needs to be beautiful, successful and happy, she comes to the conclusion that they were all wrong.

The feeling I feel with those kids is what makes me happy. Helping little kids come out of poverty makes me happy. Stretching their minds and their expectations make me happy. Why am I chasing a dream that isn't even mine?

Sam gets up fast. She has had an epiphany. Moving quickly around the house, she picks up the nearest materials she can find.

Sam yanks down her old dream board and she rips a piece of cardboard from a box. With a Sharpie in hand, she starts to draw.

She draws stick figures for adults and kids. She draws a big building. She draws a van. Then she draws two. She scribbles it out and then draws a bus. Then another.

She starts pumping more and more ideas out of her head like a pump on an oil rig. One by one, she draws up a vision, her vision.

Afterwards, she grabs her journal. Focused and anxious, she scribbles down her ideas quickly so she does not lose them.

"I am going to start a company. That company is going to take kids off of the streets in the inner city. The kids that only see crime, kids that aim for the low expectations set for them and kids whose only heroes come from a TV screen. I am going to take the athletes to the Olympics, I am going to take the future lawyers to court, I am going to take the future president to the White House, and I am going to take the fashion designers to Paris. I am going to take these kids out of here, one summer at a time and they are going to see who they can become. They are going to learn and be exposed to what life truly has to offer them.

"In my building, I am going to have computers for the future engineers. I am going to have drum sets for the future producers and video cameras for the kids who want to become filmmakers. I am going to have bestselling authors mentor the writers. I am going to have the doctors take my kids around the hospital. I am going to do this." Sam stops writing, thinks for a second, and smiles.

"And David is going to help me."

CHAPTER TWENTY SIX

From inside the elevator, David hears a loud scream. A woman is screaming on one of the floors. His heart drops, his body shakes, and he is anxious for the slow moving door to open up so he can see KG.

Finally the door opens and David walks onto the ICU floor. He sees a withering Cathy. She is barely standing as the wall seems to be holding her up. She is balling up crying. She was the one screaming.

"D! D!" That's the only words Cathy can hiccup as he moves toward her.

Immediately, David opens up his arms to embrace his sister. He holds her as she cries, shakes, and cries harder. She is sobbing, shaking her head and through the sobbing starts saying something.

"He's gone. He's gone."

David hears the words, but he's too much in shock looking through the glass at KG just lying there.

"He's gone." The words get clearer.

"He's gone," she repeats and finally it hits him.

David pulls away from Cathy and rushes to KG's bedside. KG is lying there, eyes closed like he is sleeping peacefully. The blanket is covering every inch of his brown body except for his shoulders and head.

David looks at him. He is not moving. The man who basically raised him is not moving.

"KG! KG!" David yells frantically.

David grabs his hand that's under the cover and starts shaking it.

"KG! KG! Wake up. I know you can hear me."

David lets out a loud yell. He drops down to his knees and puts his head on KG's chest. Tears stream down his face.

Cathy walks in, still crying, still seeking comfort. She tries to be strong, but bursts out into more uncontrollable sobbing.

David hears her and starts crying louder and louder. He's crying so hard, it seems like his chest can't gather in enough air.

Minutes pass and the room is eerily quiet - other than the cries of the mourning. There is no machine pumping life into KG's body, there is no heartbeat monitor dropping lines and there is nothing connecting him to any kind of life source to keep him alive. He is gone.

David stands up. He quickly wipes the tears off of his face as his expression has morphed into a hard stare. "Who did this? Who did this?"

Cathy shakes her head. "We don't know, D. We don't know."

With one last tear rolling down his face, David bends down and kisses KG on the forehead. "I love you, man. I love you."

He leaves the room while Cathy struggles to hear the words coming from his mouth.

"What? David! Where are you going?" she shouts from inside the room.

David glances back at her. "I got some business to handle."

David gets in the car with Raymond and the only words that escape his mouth are, "Take me home."

On his way back to his old neighborhood, he stares out the window while passing familiar homes, churches, and parks. He remembers the ice cream shop KG always took him to, the many talks they had there about life. He fights back the tears and thinks about Daniel. The closer they get to his house, the more focused he becomes.

Raymond drops David off at the corner of his street.

David gets out of the car. He doesn't say goodbye; he doesn't murmur a word; he just gets out, fully focused on his next move.

Like a mad man - a hit man on a mission - David plows through the back yards of all of the houses on his row, jumping gate after gate until finally he is at his house.

He doesn't want anybody to see him, especially Daniel. All he wants to do is slip into his house before his mother gets home from school, get his car, and snatch up his gun. His first stop is Sam's old house.

"Damn. You scared me," Courtney says to David, who has just walked right into her living room.

She jumps up and almost hugs him.

"What's wrong? Why are you looking so serious?" she says, jumping back.

David just stares at her sunken eyes and stringy hair. He then looks around to make sure no one else is there.

Courtney freezes. She doesn't know what to do.

"Sam doesn't live here anymore," Courtney says.

David leaves her standing dumbfounded and starts walking through the house. First, he walks through the kitchen, past the empty space where the table used to be. The same table that he and Sam used to sit down, laugh and eat at.

Then he walks around and back into the living room. The transformation amazes him.

There is no couch. Instead there are blankets and pillows at almost every corner of the room. On his way to each room, he almost trips on empty glass bottles and slips on the trash that's laid down like a thick carpet on the floor.

The place looks like a crack house for sure now. Holding his breath and trying hard not to breathe in the ratchet smell, the only thing he can do is shake his head.

Courtney sees the tall man who has added some pounds of muscle and is turned on.

With seductive eyes, Courtney studies him. He no longer looks like the snot-nosed little boy running around the neighborhood.

She likes what she sees, a man, with a goatee, a thick beard and mustache. He reminds her of Denzel Washington in *Training Day.*

Courtney slowly moves toward him. "I knew you would come to mama."

David pulls out a sandwich bag of chunky white rocks.

Her eyes buck and she immediately tries to grab it.

He pulls it back. "You know what I want."

Courtney grabs his hand and David follows.

Sam dials the number. "Tara. I mean, Ms. Peterson. Hi. This is Sam."

"Oh, hi, Sam. How have you been?" Tara asks.

A huge smile spreads across Sam's face. Hearing Tara's voice after so long brings up emotions. She really misses David.

"I was calling to see if you knew when David was getting out." Sam's heart starts racing. She is hoping for a date that is sooner rather than later.

"He's already home, sweetie."

Sam almost screams with excitement, but she holds it in.

"I came home today and his car was gone. You should come on over here. I'm about to go run to the store to get some balloons and a cake. Meet me here in, let's say, thirty minutes. I don't know where he is, but as soon as he gets back, I want to surprise him."

Sam is excited to hear that. "Okay."

Sam hangs up the phone. She starts getting her baby ready, snatches up the diaper bag, and grabs some baby food from the cabinet.

I wonder what he is going to say when he sees me. I wonder how he looks. Is he still mad? What about when he sees my baby?

Sam finishes getting her son ready and then puts on her best outfit. She fixes her hair - something she hasn't done in months - and she sprays pear body spray all over her body. She looks in the mirror and smiles.

God knows I love that boy.

After leaving Courtney's house, David speeds home, pulls up into his driveway and sits there. His eyes are red with anger and his body is bursting with adrenaline.

His gun is sitting on his lap. He is writing a letter to Sam. Tears slowly fall from his face and onto the paper as he writes. While he is looking down, he hears someone call his name.

"David?"

Startled, David throws the paper down and grabs his gun. He slides it under his shirt and then looks up to follow the direction of the sound.

"David," the voice repeats.

David turns his head, and right in front of him, walking toward his car is Jacob.

David touches his gun to make sure it's secure and then gets out of the car.

Jacob walks up on him, as if he is about to hug him, but when David puts his hand out letting him know to back up, Jacob halts.

At first, when Jacob sees him sitting there, in the car, it reminds him of the little David he used to know. But as he stands in front of the grown David, he suddenly wants to back off. Jacob immediately switches up his tone and mannerisms.

"What's up, David?" Jacob asks.

David doesn't say a word.

Jacob forces a smile, trying to read David, but is confused.

"Look, let's have a drink in my house. I wanted to talk to you about something anyway. It will only be a minute."

David follows Jacob in the house, still scanning the scene.

Once in the house, he looks at the couch and imagines Daniel sitting in the chair with Kareem, plotting the stick up. It sends a surge of anger through him. He takes in a deep breath.

"Have a seat," Jacob says extending his arm out to the chair. "Relax."

Jacob has his back turned and is pouring a shot of Scotch.

"You know that we are like family. We have history." Jacob chuckles while looking into the cabinet for another glass. "And I was surprised to hear that you were selling drugs to Sheri. She's my wife and—"

Jacob stops at the sound of metal clicking. He turns around and is met with a gun pointed at his head. Immediately, he stutters and shakes. His hands go up and his stomach drops.

"You want to talk. We can talk. No bullshit. Just straight up talk. Ya hear? Now sit the fuck down," David commands.

Jacob sits down on the couch while the pistol follows his head every inch of the way.

"Tell me, Mr. Officer. Why did you let your punk ass son rape Sam?"

Jacob's jaw drops. His mind has shut down on him. Sweat forms on his forehead.

"I'm sorry. I'm sorry." Jacob starts panicking.

"I didn't know. I was just—"

David slaps the gun across his face. Jacob's blood and tissue goes flying to the other end of the couch. His teeth are bloody and he is begging for his life.

"You wanted to talk? So talk," David yells.

With blood running down his head, Jacob sits up and tries to defend himself.

"David, I'm not perfect. I tried. We tried to raise y'all boys the best way we could. I promise you we tried…"

All of a sudden the front door opens. It's Daniel.

CHAPTER TWENTY SEVEN

Sam pulls up and parks her car right in front of Tara's front lawn, and while she is bent over, tugging at her son's car seat buckle, she hears another car pull up behind hers. Sam looks up. A great big smile instantly forms.

"Sam!" Tara yells.

With balloons and grocery bags in her hand, she runs to hug Sam. The squeeze is tight and long.

"It's so good to see you! You are so beautiful."

Sam blushes. "Thank you, ma'am," she says.

She smiles and then follows Tara into the house.

Once they get into the house, Tara looks around for David.

"David?" Tara yells as the echo of his name bounces off of the wall and comes back to her.

Sam is also confused. Her heartbeat is getting faster and faster as she is anxiously waiting for David to just pop out of a room at any moment.

"His car is outside. I wonder where he is," Tara says.

Relieved that she still has time, Tara sends Sam back out to get some tape from the store.

"I'll watch the baby," Tara says.

Sam shrugs her shoulders. "I'm with that."

As Sam leaves and shuts the door behind her, she sees someone wearing a light blue cashmere sweater and jeans walking onto the porch next door. She squints her eyes, moving forward to get a closer look. "Is that…" Sam takes a couple of more steps toward him. "That is. That's Daniel." She jogs toward him, almost running to catch up. He never looks back.

Daniel opens his front door just wide enough for her to catch a glimpse of a man standing near the doorway.

Sam's eyes focus and her head tilts. "David?"

Daniel walks right into the living room. He sees his father bleeding profusely on the couch and right there in front of him is a mad man with a gun.

Caught off guard, Daniel's hands fly up in the air. Step by step, he slowly walks to his father.

With the gun still pointed, David opens his mouth to start talking, but the door opens and Sam walks right in.

"Sam! What the hell are you doing here?" David asks.

Sam's eyes wander to the bloody man breathing heavily, and then back at David.

"What are you doing, David? You fucking crazy!"

David moves away from Sam and moves toward Daniel.

Wham. Wham. Wham. Wham.

David whacks Daniel in the skull so many times with the gun, his arm gets tired and Daniel's blood starts gushing out of his head.

Sam watches as the blood pours from his nose and ears. She screams.

"David! What's wrong with you?"

David stops hitting Daniel with the gun as his head is swelling.

"Him," David yells. He points the gun at Daniel's head, only an inch away and then slides the gun's safety button to the side. "Daniel, tell her. Tell her what you did to her," David yells.

Daniel's head is throbbing. He is moving it from side to side, trying to find even the slightest relief of pain.

Jacob looks at his bloody son and Daniel looks at his bloody father.

Jacob tries to form the words, but his lips are sore and his jaw feels like it's broken. "Tell her, son, just tell her," Jacob squeezes out.

Sam's body tenses up as she is preparing herself for the words.

Daniel's bloody eyes meet Sam's. "It was me."

"What did you do!" David grunts, digging the gun into Daniel's temples.

Daniel takes a deep breath and a hard swallow. "I…raped you."

Sam's eyes grow big. She closes them and bites her lip. A rush of images jump into her mind. She shakes her head furiously to shake the sudden pain. "No. No. No, Daniel!" Sam blocks the thoughts from further affecting her, remembering what Amina said about a person who's imprisoned by their past. She takes a deep breath and fights through the pain.

"David. It's not worth all of this. I forgave him a long time ago. God knows it was hard, but I forgave him. Life goes on. It liked to killed me, holding on to that."

Sam shakes her head and holds her hand out for the gun. "Babe, it's not worth it."

One tear falls from David's eye, while Sam tries even harder to convince him to do the right thing.

"You know all of our lives were fucked up. I know it and you know it. We ain't have the best childhood, but we can do better for our kids. But if you do this, your life is over and so is mine," she pleads.

Sam straightens her face, wipes the tears, and focuses on keeping a connection with David's softening eyes.

Step by step, Sam gets closer to David and his gun. David turns to her, puts it back on safety, and gently places the bloody metal in her hands. She grabs it. A sense of relief comes over her as she snaps open her purse. Her hands are shaking so bad it's difficult for her to find room for the bulky gun.

After successfully getting the majority of the gun in, she grabs David and turns toward the door. Just then, a gun goes off. Sam's head jerks to look back while her body instinctively ducks. David is on the floor. He is shot.

Sam falls to David. She grabs him, pulls him in toward her and rocks his limp body. Then she hears another gunshot; her body jumps to the sound. She looks up and Daniel is on the couch, slumped over. Immediately she turns to say something to Jacob to plead with him to stop, but it's too late.

Jacob looks at her, lifts the gun to his head, and pulls the trigger.

"No!" Sam screams.

At the hospital, David is in critical condition. He has tubes stuffed down his throat, taped lines of plastic along his chest, and the life support machine is pumping so hard it seems as if the air is going to make his lungs collapse. Sam looks at him lying there and can do nothing but cry. She holds his hand.

"David, I know you can hear me. I know you are there. You have to fight. You have to fight through this. Everyone is here waiting for you to wake up. We need you to get up."

Sam lifts his hand to her lips and kisses it. "I need you."

The very next day, Tara, Cathy, and Sam are waiting in the cold, white waiting room. Sam is staring at the floor, tapping her feet, waiting for the doctor to come back in, and Cathy and Tara are talking about how great of a mentor KG tried to be.

As soon as the door opens and a man with a long white coat comes walking in, everybody stops what they are doing. The grey haired doctor slowly walks toward them. His head is slightly lowered and his expression blank.

He looks at Tara and shakes his head. She nods her head back. The doctor grabs her hand as the words escape his mouth. "I'm sorry, but his condition has declined. He only has a 10 percent chance to live."

Tara lets out a cry that only a mother could produce.

"I already lost one brother. I need him," Cathy yells.

Sam doesn't say anything. She just puts her head into her cupped hands and shakes it from side to side.

Three days later, the trio is still in the waiting room, praying and waiting, praying and waiting. All day, the waiting room has been changing with new families coming up to cry and talk about their loved ones in critical condition. It is a place full of sadness and depressing stares.

Sam tries to take her mind off of David by reading a book.

"Sam," Tara says out of the blue. "I forgot. I forgot that I have something for you."

Sam looks back at her, confused. She points to her chest. "Me? You have something for me?"

Tara grabs her hand, shakes it a couple of times. "I'll go get it."

Tara returns to the waiting room with something in her hand. She is smiling - an expression that has been rare amongst the three since being in the hospital.

"Here you go, Sam," Tara says as she hands Sam a couple of notebooks and a letter.

Sam looks down at them. She stares at them trying to figure out why they look so familiar.

Her eyes widen, and her jaw drops. "My mother's journals. Where did you get this?"

Like a child seeing presents under the Christmas tree the morning of Christmas, Sam almost jumps out of her seat with excitement.

Not wanting to bring down the mood, Tara looks at Sam with droopy eyes. "I found them in David's car with this letter. I figured you might want them."

Sam's excitement drops and is soon replaced with tears.

Tara takes a seat in another section of the room.

Sam pulls out the letter David had written. She reads it, savoring every word.

Sam. I love you. And I don't ever want you to forget it. I know what happened to you and I am sorry. I am sorry how I treated you. I am sorry that I wasn't there. I'm sorry. I can never be the man that you deserve. All I know is the streets. All I know is how to survive. You deserve something better than th

As the letter abruptly ends, Sam's face scrunches. What happened to the rest of the letter? She flips the paper back and forth and back and forth as if words are going to magically appear.

She folds the paper back up and then holds it to her heart. "No. I'm sorry," she whispers to herself as if David was right there beside her.

She holds the journals in her hands, roughly wiping the dust from them. "Where did he find these?"

Sam gets up, exchanges a few words with the nurse, and then sits beside David's bed. Again, she holds his hand.

"David, you are good enough. I deserve you and you deserve me. These kids out here deserve a role model, David. You been in the streets, you've been through hurt and pain. These kids need you to show them they can make it out."

Sam's eyes wander to the heart monitor. She follows the lines with her eyes. "Who else are they going to listen to?" She rubs his hand and then runs her fingers along his face. "My son needs you. You are the perfect father for him, David. But you have to wake up. You have to fight. Your mother can't lose you. She needs you. I can't lose you. I need you. You can't—"

David interrupts her with a wiggle of his thumb. He hears her.

The wiggle is faint, but it is there.

A flow of joy runs through Sam's body. Her spirits are lifted as she starts feeling high. "I knew it. I knew." Her heart starts racing with joy as she lets go of his hand and jumps up to run and tell the others. Then the unthinkable happens. As she turns around to head out of the door, she hears a loud beeping sound. Stunned, she turns around and follows the sound.

Beep. Beep. Beep.

The sound beeps faster and faster, and then it slows. She hears more beeps coming from another machine. Then a loud alarm.

"Code blue. Code blue."

All of the blood drains from her face as she runs back over to David. "No, David! No!" she screams.

Someone grabs her, pushes her out of the room. It is the doctors and nurses. It is chaos as they fill up the tiny room.

Sam looks through the glass window as they work on David. They are moving quickly. A nurse notices her and yanks the curtains closed. Sam's legs buckle from under her. She falls to the floor.

"Don't leave me, David. Don't leave me," Sam yells. She bangs her fist against the wall. "I love you. Don't leave me!"

At the vigil, Sam sits by a tree with her burning candle and her son. Beside her is Tara and Cathy. They are crying and listening to a strong voiced woman speak to the crowd.

"We have to stop this, y'all. We have to stop the violence in our streets. The drugs are poisoning us, the guns are killing us, and the jails are profiting off of our bright young men. We have to stop it."

Sam scans the crowd and recognizes most of the young boys that are selling on the streets. Some of them she went to school with, while others she has recognized from the corner.

The woman continues. "These men are killing each other and not caring about whether they or anyone else lives or die. They have no love for each other. They have no love for themselves. We need to change it."

Sam sits there, but can't take it anymore. Something is brewing up inside and she has to let it out.

"It's you, you, you." She says pointing at the men standing around looking pitiful.

"You are who these kids see every day. They are watching you. They want to be like you. They want to look like you. Show them something different. They deserve much better than this," she says, waving at the street.

Tears run from her eyes as she gets everyone's attention. The faces are focused on her. They are knee deep into what she is saying. "Mothers, love your children. Show them how to love one another and if they don't have a father, damnit find them someone who can mentor them, someone who will influence them and guide them. It starts at home. But really it begins and ends in our own community."

A woman yells out, "Amen. It takes a village."

CHAPTER TWENTY EIGHT

Five years later.

"Come on, Junior. Hurry up. I'm 'bout tired of you and your fighting," the short woman says.

The woman grabs the ten-year old by the ear and then drags him across the street to the tall white building.

She stops at the steps. "This is it. If this doesn't work, then I don't know what to say." She narrows her eyes at her son. He tries pulling away, but she yanks him right back to her. "Don't play with me, boy," she says. He relaxes his arm, allowing her to pull him along. "All the things I do for you." She shakes her head. "I know you can do better, son. You've got to do better." With that said, she walks into the large double doors and into the building's lobby.

The air conditioning is blasting. She tightens up her jean jacket and pulls her purse in closer for warmth. At the front desk there is a woman shuffling paperwork.

The woman looks up, holds the papers in midair, and then tosses them to the side.

"Welcome," she says, standing to shake the woman's hand. My name is Ms. Peterson, but you can call me Tara. How may I serve you today, Ms...?"

Tara waits for the woman to give her a name.

"My name is Shannon." Shannon smiles at the warm hospitality. She softens her tone to a pleasant whisper.

"I was referred here by the counselor of East Mount Elementary. You see, my son has been suspended a couple of times for fighting and—"

Shannon looks at her son, who is distracted by the passing children in the hall. She bends over to the desk and whispers into Tara's ear, "Well, let's say his father isn't in his life."

Tara slowly nods her head. "Not a problem."

Shannon continues, "I was told that this was the perfect program for him."

Tara looks at the boy. "Why, yes it is. Allow me to go get our director." Tara points to a couch. "Please, have a seat."

As Tara walks to the back, Shannon stretches her neck to observe every little thing in the building. There are plaques, there are certificates, and there are dozens of pictures of professional men and women as well as others mentoring children. "Wow," Shannon says. She turns around to check the wall behind her. Right above her head is another plaque. She stands up to check it out more. It is the key to the City of East Mount. "Wow. This is such a nice place." Shannon looks at her son. "I sure hope we can get you in here."

Suddenly, a loud clacking of shoes echoes through the hallway. The sound comes closer and closer until a woman appears. Standing tall in front of her is a woman with a strong presence. She is wearing a white business suit with a rose colored blouse peeking out. On her finger is a small sparkling wedding ring. The woman walks with her head up, shoulders back, and her voice is welcoming, yet strong.

"Hello, Ms. Shannon, my name is Samantha and I will help you further."

Samantha then kneels down to the little boy. He smiles at her.

"Well, hi there. You can call me Sam. What's your name?"

The boy looks at her, mesmerized by her stunning beauty.

"My name is David."

"David, huh?" She chuckles. "Awesome name." She extends her hand to shake his.

"Follow me. I will show you around."

The woman and her son follow Sam through the building. Their eyes are wide and their mouths are open wider. They can't believe what they are seeing.

"So, I see you like music," Sam says pointing at the boy's Michael Jackson t-shirt.

David doesn't say anything. He just smiles.

Shannon nudges him with her purse.

David grabs his aching arm.

"You better speak up," his mother tells him.

"Yeah. I want to play the piano, like Elton John."

Samantha looks back at the boy, surprised. "What you know about Elton John?" She gives him a big smile.

Shannon speaks up. "Oh. I've been playing Elton ever since he was in my stomach."

Sam continues to walk down the hall. She begins to sing, "B-b-b-benny and the j-e-ts."

A burst of laughter comes out of David. He smiles and looks at his mother.

Shannon turns to him with an even bigger smile as she pulls him in closer to her.

271

"Well, you will love it here. Let me show you our studio," Sam says.

They walk past a large glass window that shows a room with a long workstation, a soundproof booth, and chairs lined up around it. There is a man standing up and teaching the children.

"Is that the studio?" David looks around, mesmerized by the equipment. He has only seen a studio on *MTV Cribs*.

"Yes, sir. It is," Sam says.

"How much is this place? I was told it was free," Shannon says, nervous that she can't afford it.

Sam looks at her with a smile.

"Oh, it is. Everything in this facility is free. From the trips, the classes, to the meals. We pride ourselves on having the largest number of sponsors and mentors in the state. All of the classes are taught by professionals. They are all given a thorough background check and they all donate their time and skills."

Sam leads them into a room on the right.

"Now here is the library."

Sam walks around the room filled with bookshelves upon bookshelves of books. They are all labeled according to specific interests.

"From golf to how to patent an invention, it is all here. We want our children to have access to any subject they want to learn more about. We will even special order books depending on the specific needs of a child. I have a couple of children that are reading college books because they are at that level. Daily reading is mandatory here at the program."

She points to a woman who is wearing a pair of khakis and a rainbow colored sweater. "This is my son's grandmother." Sam pats her shoulders. "This woman right here has a story. A story that she often shares with the children here. We all have a story. But it's the ending that counts."

Next, Sam stops in front of a clear case. She lays her hand on it and admires the lights shining on her most prized possession. "This right here is how this all came about. My mother left me with more advice on life than one could ever wish for. To this day, I will go back and look for answers to everyday situations. It is a constant reminder to students to always seek guidance from their parents. We've been there. So most of the time, we are the best people to get advice from."

Sam glances down at the case. "Our parents will not always be here."

They leave the library and continue down another hallway. As they walk, they see artwork for sale from the kids that attend the center and also outfits that were hand sewn from the children as well. "We also have an entrepreneurial program here."

Shannon raises her eyebrow in disbelief. "This place is unbelievable."

Sam smiles. "Believe it."

From there they begin to walk into a couple of different rooms. Every room has its own specific theme. The photography room has cameras, backdrops, and students who are developing their pictures. The fashion room is filled with kids as young as eight on sewing machines. Some are trying different styles on the mannequins.

Shannon looks at Sam and says, "I wish I had it good like this. Y'all doing it big in here. You just don't know."

Sam lets out a chuckle. "No. You just don't know. Trust me."

Suddenly, a boy runs up to Sam and grabs her legs, almost knocking her down. He tugs at her top.

"Hey, son," Sam says. "Go and ask grandma to round up all of the kids so they can get ready to get on the bus."

Sam turns back around to Shannon, who is looking sad that the tour is over.

"Well, that is the end of the tour. We would love to have you here. All you have to do is fill out some paperwork letting us know more about David and his interests and aspirations in life and we can go from there. It was nice meeting you, Shannon." Sam shakes the woman's hand, gripping it firmly. Then she kneels down to David. "We would love to have you here. But you have to mind your mother, okay?"

David nods his head.

"All right, children," Sam says to the long line of kids. "Is everyone here?"

"Yes!"

Sam leads them onto the bus. They take the longest route. It's the most scenic route with all of the beautiful houses and upscale businesses lined up on each street. Sam points to one of the white stone buildings. "That's where we will be taking a group of kids tomorrow," she says to the bus driver.

The bus driver reads the lit up sign, "Cathy and Associates Law Firm. Yes, ma'am."

Sam smiles.

"This can be you one day. If you work hard and work on your craft every day, this can be you," Sam says while making her way through the aisles.

Finally, the bus slows down.

"We're here," Sam says. All she can see is the kids jumping up and down in their seats like they have just been charged up with sugar.

They pull up into a big beautiful parking lot with a huge sign. It reads, "Khalil Grant's Fine Dining."

The kids cheer. They are so excited. It is the dream of every last one of them to become famous chefs.

One little boy is almost in tears as he remembers being told that cooking isn't for boys. He smiles at the sign. His heart beats fast at the opportunity to actually do something he loves to do.

They unload the bus and then head to the door.

They are met by a tall man in a white chef's hat and a white apron tied around his waist.

"Welcome," the man says in a deep masculine voice.

Sam looks at her husband standing there, looking sexier than ever. She watches him smile at the kids and wave his hand for them to join him in the kitchen.

"David," she yells.

He turns around. "Yes, babe?"

She smiles. "Nothing, I just wanted to see you smile again."

David laughs and hurries to catch the children before they touch anything with their unwashed hands.

"The first thing you want to do is wash your hands," David says.

One by one, the children wash their hands. David shows them the proper way to wash from the wrist down to their fingernails. He even sings with them his tweaked version of the "Happy Birthday" song.

From the dining room, Sam watches it all. She sits down with her three month old cradled in her arms and begins to feed him. "Junior, look at your father. He's that dude."

She looks up and admires her husband even more as she watches him help the kids put on their aprons and properly set the table. "The salad fork belongs here," David says.

He takes a second and looks back over at Sam. Showing his teeth, he smiles at her and winks. He mouths the words, "I love you."

Sam winks back. She blushes, smiling from ear to ear. "I love you, too."

It only takes one person to change a life.

FREE Sneak Peek of THE INFLUENCED TWO COMING SOON!

http://www.khadijagrant.com

THANK YOU!

PLEASE SUPPORT! Submit a review on <u>Amazon</u> , <u>Goodreads</u> and <u>*Facebook*</u> at KhadijaGrantBooks, or even your blog! It will do wonders for my writing career.

If you really enjoyed the book, please call a friend, tweet about the book, or even lend the book to someone who may enjoy it.

Contact me personally at khadijagrant.com and thank you again for all the love and support!

Best Wishes,

Khadija Grant

BOOKS BY KHADIJA GRANT

You Can Start One Too!

Plant seeds of entrepreneurship at any age.

A young girl travels around the city with her father and discovers that she can own a business, too. All she has to do is envision it and plan it. This book is a seed worth planting in your child's imagination. One that will inspire them to imagine owning their own business as well as motivate them to start planning right now.

Release date is March 2016.

THE ITCH

A young boy gets chased into the woods by bullies. They escape without a scratch, but he is not as fortunate. Or is he? An inspirational book for young children full of suspense, mystery and morals about money and friendship. This book is a classic page-turner for anyone who loves a story with morals.

Release date is March 2016

Made in the USA
Middletown, DE
21 December 2017